Vicious Circle. Act One.

Jordan Simpson

Copyright 2023

ISBN: 978-1-7389997-0-5

Interior - Day - Restaurant

As the scene fades in from black, we see a dimly lit restaurant, it is old fashioned early80's truck stop vibe. Standing with his back turned to the camera is a young man who is waiting on a customer. We do not see who he is talking to.

Waiter:

What can I get you?

The voice of a young teenager can be heard although still not seen.

Teenager:

Just a salad and a drink please.

Waiter:

What kind of dressing would you like with your salad?

Teenager:

It doesn't matter.

Waiter:

(Sighing) Ok Greek it is. That'll be twelve dollars. Would you like that here or to go?

Teenager:

Here's fine.

The restaurant is filled at half capacity, scattered with old and young people alike. They all take turns looking at the ongoing conversation between the customer and waiter. There is mumbling and looks of shock, disgust and awe. Suddenly a little girl (6) is seen with her mother. She points to the customer and exclaims loudly.

Child:

Mommy, why does that girls face look like that?

Mother:

(Trying to get her daughter to turn around). Would you sit down and stop starring.

Child:

(Turning around). She's hideous.

Mother:

Eat your food sweetie.

Child:

Did she get into an accident? (Turning back around). Hey lady did you get into an accident?

Suddenly the camera turns back to the customer. We now see her face. She is hideously deformed. She is blind in her left eye; her nose is missing and instead there is just a flat canvas of skin with a slit in it for her to breathe. Her lips are missing, and cheeks are sunken in.

Teenager:

(Louder with intensity with every word). Stop looking at me. Stop looking at me. Stop looking at me. I know what I look like. You think I chose to look like this? You think I chose this? This life? I know what i look like. I'm reminded everyday of what I look like. So stop looking at me.

She turns to look at the waiter. The waiter has taken a step back, a concerned look across his face. People have their cellphones and are recording the situation.

Teenager:

I know you look at me like I'm some sort of freak. You think I wanted this; you think I asked for this. Well, I don't need your sympathy. What I need is my fucking life back.

Without missing a beat, she beings to start pounding her face off the table. Blood beings to pour down the top of her forehead.

Teenager (continued):

I... Want.... My.... Fucking.... Life... Back!

The waiter jumps back in horror as the teenager continues to bash her face off the table. Some good Samaritans jump up to pull her away from the table others call 911. As they wrestle with her the camera zooms in on the table. Placed in the middle of a blood pool is a single tooth.

Fade Out.

MONTAGE - SCHOOL HALL

As the scene opens there are glimpses of a high school setting. People in halls are being pushed around and bullied.

-- In the halls three bullies surround a young man, they have him on the ground kicking him. He lies curled up in the fetal position, crying and pleading.

-- Girls outside in the soccer fields are fighting, grabbing and pulling hair.

-- Groups of kids' corner a young man in the washroom, they grab
him and hold in upside down in the toilet.

-- Teenagers corner students behind the school, knocking books
out of their hands. Spiting in their faces.

-- Young man sits at home crying; he runs a straight razor across
his wrist.

-- A girl swallows Oxycontin, crying out her sorrow in the
bathroom.

-- A mother picks her daughter up off the floor, pukes running
down the girls' face. The mother pleads for her to wake up.

-- A group of kids walk into a school, guns loaded, and they begin
to fire rounds at students and teachers as they walk into the
classrooms.

-- A television screen of a news report states there has been
another teen suicide or another school shooting.

-- Parents at funerals crying, standing over as their child's
coffin is lowered into the ground.

-- Students in gymnasiums mourn the loss of fellow students, as
pictures of their classmates are played out on a screen. A
tribute to the fallen.

-- Halls of the school, kids are still being picked on and pushed
around.

Back to scene.

INT. BLAKES HOUSE - BEDROOM - SECOND FLOOR - NIGHT.

BLAKE sits alone on his bed, a lamp on his desk is the only light
that illuminates the room. His room is well kept, shoes are
sorted out on a shoe rack by his door. His room has several
posters, all of men. From Taylor Lautner to Justin Bieber. His
clothes are clean pressed and hung up in the closet. Blake Gilmore
is a well-dressed man for his age.

He is roughly around the age of 17, his graduation pictures are
lying on his desk. There are multiple pictures on his proof sheet.
Blakes hair is blond with blue streaks. Both of his ears are
pierced as well as his bottom lip.

He is sitting on the edge of his bed, his head held in his hands.
Tears are dripping out past the cracks in his fingers. A folded-
up letter is placed on his pillow, the paper is tear stained. He
reaches under his bed and pulls out an old shoe box. He places it
on the bed beside him and pulls out an old colt single action
revolver.

He checks the chamber: it's empty. He quickly rummages through the
box and finds a single bullet. He places it into the chamber and
closes it. With a spin of the chamber, he holds the gun to his
head. He presses it tightly against the side of his head. He
mutters a silent prayer and pulls the trigger.

Click.

The gun didn't go off, he's playing Russian roulette with himself.
He places the gun back onto the side of the bed and starts to
hyperventilate. He's trying to work up the courage to do it again.
He does.

Click.

Still the gun doesn't go off. He is about to try for a third time
when he hears a loud crash coming from downstairs.
There is someone hollering and shouting, his FATHER has just come
home from being out.

                    FATHER:
          Where are you, you little faggot? I know
          your home from school.

Blake places the gun quickly back into the box and back under his
bed. He reaches for the door to lock it, but his father has
already stumbled up the stairs and burst through the door. The
door swings up and catches Blake in the face, cracking his nose.
Blood seeps out onto his rugged floor.

(CONTINUED)

CONTINUED:

                    FATHER:
          Look at you, all alone up in your room
          crying. Being a little girlie bitch huh,
          I always said you were just like your
          mom. Couldn't take a beating either.

Blake falls back onto his bed, as his father drunkenly stumbles
towards him. He starts to undo his belt and readies it in his
hands. Blake cowers on his bed.

                    BLAKE:
          Dad you're drunk, just go to bed.

                    FATHER:
          Go to bed! Who the fuck are you to tell
          me what to do. Just like your whore
          mother.

He swings the belt down, metal part first, across Blakes face.
Blake clenches his face at the welt that is now growing. His
dad swings the belt at him again.

                    BLAKE:
          Ow, stop it dad stop it.

                    FATHER:
          Stop what? I'll stop it when you learn to
          be a man. You're a Gilmore start acting
          like one. Men need to learn to be
          strong, to stand up against their
          enemy's. Now stand up.

                    BLAKE:
          You're hurting me, stop it dad.

                    FATHER:
          Your mother would say the same thing. She
          never did change, always just laid there
          on her back. But a whore would be used to
          that, fucked more men than she fucked me.
          Left me with a son, just like her.
          Fucking loves the cock. No son of mine is
          going to be a faggot. Now you man up and
          start acting like one.

He hits Blake several more times before he stumbles out of the
room. Blake crawls to his door and closes it, he takes a white t-
shirt from his closet and wipes blood from his face and hands. He
clears the tears up from his eyes and sits down at his desk and
flips open his computer.

INSERT - COMPUTER

The screen opens and he quickly logs into Facebook, his Facebook
profile picture is a picture of him and another student, DEREK
GRANT. The picture of them is at school, they're smiling and got
an arm around each other's neck. It would appear to be a normal
photo of two buddies; however Blake had crafted the photo so that
the two of them were centered into the middle of a heart.

His Facebook has several notifications, he continues to view them
all. Peoples' comments on the photo, hurtful words from people
directed towards him.

-- Mike Theodore: "What a fag, wait until Derek sees this."

-- Chris Cook: "We need less of your kind in this world, Kill
yourself."

-- Serena Matthews: "It's Adam and Eve dear, not Adam and Steve.
The bible hates people like you."

One of the notifications directs him to a page, created by
someone anonymous. It's entitled "*Please share. Every like gets
Blake Gilmore one step closer to killing himself.*" There are
pictures that someone drew on of him, with phallic symbols marking
them everywhere.

Blake slams the computer and starts crying again, not before a
burst of rage makes him scale his computer across the room. He
takes the letter from his pillow and shreds it.
Beginning to write a new letter, he grabs a piece of paper and
frantically begins to write several individuals' names.

INT. STACY LAWERENCE'S HOUSE - BEDROOM - SAME.

Stacy is a 17-year-old girl, flowing blond hair. She dresses up in
fashion, her room is also covered in boy posters. Her
cheerleading costume hangs by the door, her room is in complete
disarray, she is in the state of mind of a person who no longer
cares. Her MOTHER calls out to her from down the hall.

                    MOTHER:
          Stacy sweetie supper is ready. Come and
          get it.

Stacy lays on her floor in silence, staring up at the ceiling fan
as it spins around. She is lost in her own little world, but she
soon slowly sits up. She looks at her bedroom door.

CONTINUED:

                    STACY:
          In a minute mom, I'll be down in a
          minute.

                    MOTHER:
          Ok, but don't be too long, supper will
          get cold.

Stacy sits on her bed and opens her tablet. She is scrolling
through her emails until she comes across one and stops.

INSERT - COMPUTER

The subject line reads "Check out this whore" and embedded into the
email is a video. However, the email isn't lit up like an unread
message, this email is several days old.
Stacy clicks the video and opens it. She turns the volume on her
tablet down to a dull roar. The video begins to play.

The camera comes on to show a video of Stacy herself, she is being
forced backwards in someone's room until she falls on her back
onto the bed. Three MEN appear into the screen with her, they are
all shirtless wearing masks over their faces. One is wearing a
rabbit mask, the other a wolf, and the other a sheep. Their faces
are unidentifiable. The man behind the camera speaks first. He
points to the sheep and the wolf.

                    MAN BEHIND THE CAMERA:
          You two hold her down, try to get her
          undressed without her kicking and
          screaming.

The man in the wolf mask takes off one of his socks and stuffs it
in her mouth. She tries to fight them, but she is too drunk to
move. Her kicks are too weak. They take of her pants and shirt,
leaving her in her undergarments. All three of them are slowly
slipping out of their own pants themselves. The camera zooms in on
her face, she is crying, mascara smeared down her face.

                    MAN BEHIND THE CAMERA:
          Smile for the camera baby girl, you're
          going to be a star.

Stacy tries to scream past the sock in her mouth, as the camera
zooms out showing the man in the rabbit mask about to get on top of
her. Stacy pauses the film and turns off the tablet. There comes a
knock at her door.

                                              (CONTINUED)

CONTINUED:

                    MOTHER:
          Sweetie, are you OK in there? Your supper
          is getting cold.

Stacy jumps up and greets her at the door., she has a fake smile on
her face.

                    STACY:
          Ya I'll be there in a minute I said,
          I just need to go to the bathroom and
          freshen up.

                    MOTHER:
          Ok well as long as you're OK in there,
          you've been very distant lately. You'd
          tell me if there was something wrong
          wouldn't you?

                    STACY:
          Yes, mother I would, but there's nothing
          to worry about.

Her mother gives her a hug and gently kisses her on the forehead.

                    MOTHER:
          As your mother I must worry, but if you
          say there's nothing wrong then I believe
          you. Now hurry up, I'll go pop your food
          in the microwave.

Stacy walks to the bathroom and closes the door, then looks at
herself in the mirror before reaching into the medicine cabinet
and opening a can of prescribed pills. She pops a few into her
hand and places the bottle back where it belongs.

INT. MIRANDA OSTEEN'S HOUSE - BATHROOM - SAME.

MIRANDA (18) is standing alone in her bathroom, looking at
herself in the mirror. She has long black hair, and she picks up
a brush and begins to comb it. She starts out slowly but soon
picks up speed pulling at the knots in her hair when the comb
gets caught. She drops the comb and begins to rip at the hair
with her hands.

She rummages through the cabinets until she pulls out a first aid
kit. She dumps the contents on the floor and picks out a pair of
safety scissors. The kind used for cutting bandages or tape. She
takes a lock of her hair and uses dull scissors to cut it. She
takes off several locks, her

hair now looks like someone went through it with a lawnmower. She
screams into the mirror.

                    MIRANDA:
          Fuck you, fuck you, fuck you. You ugly
          worthless piece of shit.
          Everybody hates you because you look
          like a pig. You disgust everyone around
          you. 'Oh, look its Miranda the walrus.'
          'Hey did you hear there was another
          earthquake in China today, that Miranda
          must have fallen out of bed again.'

She lifts her shirt to expose her belly in the mirror, she isn't
a big woman that she makes herself to be. She takes the dull
scissors at tries to cut at her stomach, but this is to no avail.
She tosses the scissors to the floor. Without warning she smashes
the mirror with her fist, shards break and fall to the sink
counter. She grabs the biggest shard she can find and begins to
run it across her stomach. Blood starts to seep out of the cuts,
the marks she leaves aren't serious enough to require medical
attention.

                    MIRANDA:
          Curse you for being born this way.

She tosses the glass into the garbage and begins to doctor up her
cuts. Once done she kneels by the toilet, she lifts the lid and
puts her head in. She puts two fingers deep into her throat and
begins to vomit.

INT. BRIAN MONROE'S HOUSE - LIVING ROOM - SAME.

Brian (18) is in his living room, but this isn't an ordinary
living room. Besides the normal television stand with tv, the
couches have all been moved over into one corner. Taken up most
space is a bow flex exercise gym, complete with all the
accessories. There is also a treadmill, and weights.

Brian is a frail teenager; his body is built tall but lanky. He
has no muscle to his frame, but he sits there on his workout bench
doing butterflies. The weight is currently set at 40 pounds. He
stops from his workout and uses his shirt to wipe the sweat from
his brow. He gets up and walks to the kitchen where he makes
himself a whey protein powder shake and drinks it down.

His father walks in through the front door, he is dressed in a
police officer uniform. He takes off his jacket and vest and
places them on the table. He takes his side arm and baton and
places them on the table as well.

CONTINUED:

                    OFFICER MONROE:
          I see you've been working up a sweat in
          here. Think you're making any progress?

                    BRIAN:
          I think so, I'm excited for tomorrow. I'm
          going to go try out for the football
          team. Got a good feeling about it this
          time.

                    OFFICER MONROE:
          Well if you think you're ready. I don't
          want to see you out there getting hurt
          again.

Brian flexes his muscles.

                    BRIAN:
          This right here dad, this is the gun
          show. Ladies are going to love it when
          they see me out there on that field. By
          tomorrow afternoon, I'm officially going
          to be one of the cool kids.

His father laughs at him, he then picks up his gun and baton and
carries them down to the basement. Brian follows him down the
stairs, where they stop at a safe. It is a large combination
safe, about 7 feet tall, large enough to hold two people.

Brian watches him as he turns the dial. 11-23-15. The safe opens
and his father places his gun and baton inside. There is also
another bullet proof vest, several boxes of live ammunition and
two Browning 12-gauge semi-automatic shotguns. His father closes
the safe and locks it. He turns back towards his son.

                    OFFICER MONROE:
          Don't be doing this just because you
          feel the need to be popular. You're not
          that type of kid.

                    BRIAN:
          If I can't be popular, then who can I
          be?

                    OFFICER MONROE:
          You can be yourself, all you need to be
          is yourself.

His father goes to head back upstairs, but he stops at the bottom
step.

CONTINUED:

                    OFFICER MONROE:
          If you think you're strong enough to try
          out for a football team, maybe your
          strong enough to finally try out the
          shotgun I bought you.

                    BRIAN:
          You mean it?

                    OFFICER MONROE:
          Sure do, maybe later this week we can go
          down to the range. Put a couple holes
          into them tin cans they got out there.
          That's providing that you're sure that
          you're strong enough that the gun won't
          knock you on your ass this time.

                    BRIAN:
          I'm sure dad, you'll see come tomorrow
          I'll be lead quarterback on the
          Silvercreek Highs football team.

                    OFFICER MONROE:
          We'll see then won't we.

His father continues to walk up the stairs, leaving Brian in the
basement alone. Brian eyes the safe for a moment, he takes his
time before heading back upstairs.

EXT. SILVERCREEK HIGH - MORNING.

Buses are arriving at the school on time, kids are jumping out
and meeting up with friends. A black 2008 Honda accord pulls into
the school student parking lot, Brian is sitting by his father.
Brian is dressed up in his football gear and uniform, his father
is dressed up and ready for work.

                    OFFICER MONROE:
          Goodluck today on the tryouts, I'll see
          you later tonight after work, you can
          tell me how you did then.

                    BRIAN:
          Maybe tonight we can go out and get
          pizza, celebrate.

CONTINUED:

                    OFFICER MONROE:
          Sounds like a plan to me.

He gives Brian a hug, tears start to fill his eyes.

                    OFFICER MONROE: (CONT'D)
          Your mother would be so proud if she
          could see you now.

                    BRIAN:
          She is proud of both of us dad, and she's
          watching down on you and me.

His father pulls away and wipes away his tears.

                    OFFICER MONROE:
          You're right, she is. OK you better get
          going if you don't want to be late. Good
          luck, show them who's boss.

                    BRIAN:
          Will do.

Brian gets out of the car and heads towards the football field. The
bell to start classes has rung.

EXT. FOOTBALL FIELD - CONTINUOUS.

Brian has joined the rest of the team and they are lined up in
the center of the field. Coach JOEL SIMMONS (35-40) is drilling
the team when Brian finally shows up. On the opposite side of the
field the cheerleading squad can be seen performing their tryouts
as well.

                    MR. SIMMONS:
          Well look who finally showed up to the
          tryouts everybody. You must be Mr.
          Monroe; tell me Monroe do you think you
          have what it takes to be a part of the
          team?

Brian forms a position beside the others and dons on his helmet.
Compared to the others Brian is a toothpick.

                    BRIAN:
          Yes, sir I think I do.

Everyone in the lineup starts to snicker, even Mr. Simmons.

                                                        (CONTINUED)

CONTINUED:

                    MR. SIMMONS:
          And enlighten us, why do you think you
          have what it takes to be a part of my
          team?

                    BRIAN:
          Because I am a team player, I'm always in
          it to win it. It's either go big or go
          home.

By this time everyone has cracked up laughing, MIKE THEODORE
(18) is the first person to speak up.

                    MIKE:
          Team player? More like a team punching
          bag, just look at the size of you. You're
          going to be tossed around and out,
          you'll never even make it to the first
          game.

His buddies CHRIS COOK (17), HENRY RUSH (17) and JOHN ADAMS
(17) are now all chiming in with their insults.

                    CHRIS:
          Go home pipsqueak.

                    JOHN:
          Dying children in Africa have more muscle
          than you.

                    HENRY:
          Go big or go home, OK then go home.

Mr. Simmons is raising his hands to quiet the boys down, Brian
stands there and takes it all in. He doesn't let it bother him.

                    MR. SIMMONS:
          Enough, enough. Let's just see how well
          Mr. Monroe here can handle himself out
          in the field.
          Gentlemen let's play some ball.

The boys square off in the field, getting into positions. Mr.
Simmons holds back Mike, while the others get ready.

                    MR. SIMMONS:
          Show Brian there what it takes to really
          play football, make him hurt.

CONTINUED:

                    MIKE:
          Will do coach.

He joins the rest of the team, but not before huddling in a group
with Chris, John and Henry. He whispers something in their ears,
and they nod, they come to join the rest of the team.

Game is ready, set and they're off. Brian is running down the
field, he's open. A team member of his tosses him the ball, he
catches he's running for a touchdown when out of nowhere Mike
crashes into Brian's body slamming him into the ground. Mike gets
off him.

                    MIKE:
          Wooooo, damn. You just got owned son.

Brian catches his breath but he's not done yet he stands up and
is ready for more.

                    BRIAN:
          Is that all you got big guy.

                    MIKE:
          So little man wants some more eh, lets
          show him boys.

Before Brian can turn around Chris tackles him from behind, John
and Henry pile on top. They get off him, but this time Brian
doesn't get up he lays there on the field, moaning to soar to
move. His arm is dislocated.

The coach motions two PLAYERS to pick him up off the field.

                    MR. SIMMONS:
          Bring that big baby here and off the
          field, let the real boy's play.

One of the players speaks up when he helps Brian to his feet.

                    PLAYER #1:
          Ah coach, I think his arm has been
          dislocated.

                    MR. SIMMONS:
          Bring him here, I'll set his arm and then
          you two can take him back to the locker
          room.

CONTINUED:

The two players bring him over to the coach, the coach grabs hold
of his arm and shoves up. There is a loud pop and Brian screams.

                    MR. SIMMONS:(CONT'D)
              There you go, now get off my field this
              isn't a place for babies and pussies.

The two players escort Brian back to the locker room, from the
top of the field Mike can be heard shouting.

                    MIKE:
              I guess he chose to go home.

INT. SCHOOL LOCKER ROOM - CONTINUOUS.

The room is a pale blue color, benches Aline the middle of the
room and lockers on either side. There are showers, sinks and
toilets at the back of the room.

Brian is rubbing his arm, swinging it back and forth wincing at the
pain. He has gotten out of his uniform and into his normal
clothes, blue jeans, Nike shoes and dress shirt. He has finished
putting away his uniform when the door to the locker room opens.
In comes Mike and his buddies.

                    MIKE:
              Look boys it's the crybaby, how's the
              arm treating you?

The boys corner Brian up against the lockers. There is no way for
him to escape.

                    BRIAN:
              Arms fine. Now if you excuse me, I must
              be going.

Brian tries to push past them, but Mike pushes him back against
the locker.

                    MIKE:
              Wow, now hold up, don't be like that. We
              just want to talk.

                    BRIAN:
              About what?

                    MIKE:
              Anything really. You know I seen you
              earlier today, sitting in the car with
              your dad. Must be so proud

                         (MORE)

                                             (CONTINUED)

MIKE: (cont'd)
> of you. Saw him cry you know, what is
> it? Big cop can't handle his little boy
> growing up. Or was it something else, oh
> I know. Maybe he was finally realizing
> that his son is a failure and would
> never make it on the football team just
> like he can't make it as a cop. You do
> know your father is a failure right, I
> mean even the other cops pick on him at
> work. The only reason he got to the
> position he's in is because your mother
> died.

The other boys begin to chuckle.

> BRIAN:
> Leave my father out of this.

> MIKE:
> Why? You going to hit me, I know you
> want to. I see the way you looked at me
> out on the field there. Oh, how I wanted
> to do so much more to you, but the coach
> only wanted me to rough you up out there.
> I wanted to break your back, like I did
> to your dead mother when I rode her
> fucking ass off.

Brian has finally had enough; he lets loose and cracks Mike across
the face. Big mistake.

> JOHN:
> OOOOOHHH, that was a bad idea. What are
> you going to do to him? Want us to teach
> him another lesson.

> MIKE:
> Calm down boys, I think I know exactly
> what to do with him. Seems someone
> doesn't like people talking about his
> dead mother, I bet you she's riding up
> the big old cock in hell. Maybe that's
> why your dad is so upset, couldn't even
> as a cop protect his own wife maybe he's
> afraid something bad will happen to his
> son too. Well lets show him boys, here
> it seems we have got a fighter, well
> lets show his dad what his fighter is
> made of.

CONTINUED:

                    MIKE: (cont'd)
          Hey who knows, maybe he'll have a heart
          attack and die, wouldn't that be nice.

The boys proceed to punch and kick Brian, knocking out at least
two of his teeth and breaking his nose. They are in the middle of
kicking him when Mr. Simmons walks into the room. They turn and
stop.

                    MR. SIMMONS:
          What seems to be going on here?

                    MIKE:
          We were just fooling around with our
          old pal Brian here. Talking about how he
          took that tackle like a champ.

                    MR.SIMMONS:
          Mr. Theodore I'll have you know that any
          roughhousing is to remain on the field
          it will not be tolerated in the school
          itself.

With that, Mr. Simmons turns his back on the boys.

                    MR. SIMMONS:(CONT'D)
          With that being said just pretend like
          we're still on the field.

The boys take that as a sign and continue to beat down on Brian.
They then pick him up and drag him to the showers where they turn
them on and let him soak in the water.

                    MIKE:
          Clean yourself off, you look like shit.

The coach and the boys walk out of the locker room leaving Brian
all alone.

EXT. FOOTBALL FIELD - SAME.

Miranda is walking along the field towards the cheerleader
tryouts. She stops to look out the corner of her eye towards the
football team. The team has just formed up and is beginning to
play.

                    MIRANDA:
          Damn those boys are cute, once those boys
          see me though they won't

                         (MORE)

                                                    (CONTINUED)

CONTINUED:

                    MIRANDA: (cont'd)
          have time to play their eyes will be too
          busy watching me.

One of the boys (Brian), although she can't quite see who it is,
gets tackled and taken down. Miranda winces at the sight of it.

                    MIRANDA:(CONT'D)
          Stuff like that is going to constantly be
          happening once they get a load of my new
          body.

Miranda walks up to the team of cheerleaders and takes off her
backpack. She pulls out a Tupperware container filled with
cookies and hands them over to the coach MRS. MARGRET KING (30).

Miranda stands before the team dressed in all black attire. She is
wearing a winter hat on her head. The girls all started laughing
at her. SERENA MATTHEWS (18) is the first to speak up.

                    SERENA:
          Look, it's the elephant, who let you out
          of the zoo you ugly elephant?

                    MRS.KING:
          Now ladies there is no need to be mean
          with Mrs. Osteen here. I'm sure she has a
          good reason to come back.

KELSEY MOORE (17) and JENNIE MILES(18), finally speak up as well.

                    KELSEY:
          Maybe she's here to tryout again for the
          team.

                    JENNIE:
          I didn't know we let animals join our
          team.

Miranda starts to cry but wipes away her tears.

                    MIRANDA:
          I was thinking about trying out for the
          team again. I did as you said, I worked
          out making myself skinny overnight.

CONTINUED:

                    SERENA:
          Sweetie, you don't just get skinny
          overnight, a body like mine takes
          perfection. It's a master skill that
          takes time to craft. Those cookies
          surely aren't going to help you get any
          less fat.

                    MIRANDA:
          But I bought these for all of you to
          enjoy, a sign of good faith.

                    JENNIE:
          Honey, we take your cookies, but we all
          know you want to eat them all for
          yourself.

The coach hands the cookies back to Miranda. She raises a hand to
silence the girls.

                    MRS.KING:
          Girls that's enough, there's a time and
          place for everything and right now isn't
          the time. Now Miranda, I told you once
          you didn't have what it takes to be on
          the team, and clearly you still don't.
          Now take your cookies and get off the
          field, obviously baking is more your
          style.

                    MIRANDA:
          But the team, I just want to be a part of
          it. I want to be able to fit in, to be
          one of you.

                    SERENA:
          At no point in life will you ever be one
          of us. Go home hippo.

                    MRS.KING:
          You know what, if you're so eager to stay
          and try out then so be it. Get your
          uniform and prepare.

Miranda looks around confused.

                    MIRANDA:
          I don't have a uniform though; do you
          think you have an extra my size.

                                              (CONTINUED)

CONTINUED:
                    MRS.KING:
          No uniform! So, you come here unprepared
          and expect to tryout.

                    MIRANDA:
          I wasn't expected to have one the last
          time.

Mrs. King is about to tell Miranda to leave again when she looks to
her left to see someone coming down the field.

                    MRS.KING:
          Oh, look ladies, Mrs. Lawrence has
          finally shown up to practice.

                    STACY:
          I'm not here to stay, I'm here to say I
          quit. Here's my uniform.

She tosses her uniform into Miranda's hands.

                    STACY:(CONT'D)
          Looks like you could use this, take it
          its yours.

                    MIRANDA:
          Thanks.

Stacy walks off the field and out of earshot.

                    SERENA:
          Where does that whore think she's going?

                    KELSEY:
          Teams better off without that slut
          skanking up the place.

                    MRS.KING:
          Girls, as hard as it is to see one of
          your fellow cheermasters walk away, you
          should still be keeping strong
          passionate memories about them. Now,
          Miranda looks like it's your lucky day.
          Get dressed and let's see what you got.

Miranda turns her back to the team and undresses in the middle of
the field. By this time the boys' football has already walked off
the field and back to classes. Miranda puts on the cheerleading
uniform, it's too tight for her but she manages to make it fit.

She turns back towards her team, her hat however still on.

CONTINUED:
                         MRS.KING:
            Miranda, I need you to take off your hat.

                         MIRANDA:
            I can't, I sorry. Can't I just try out
            with it on.

                         MRS.KING:
            I'm sorry I need you to take it off.

                         SERENA:
            Do it, take it off.

                         JENNIE:
            Take it off.

                         KELSEY:
            Take it off.

The other girls are cheering for her to take off her hat, Miranda
is hesitant, but she slowly rips of her hat exposing her new
haircut.

The girls all stared shocked and they begin to laugh, even the
coach.

                         JENNIE:
            Did you get in a fight with a
            bushwhacker? What happened to your hair?

Miranda just stands there speechless, at this point her shirt
finally comes up starting to expose the some of her belly. Now
the girls just stare at her disgusted at the marks on her
stomach.

                         SERENA:
            You have issues that you need to sort out
            before you can ever join our team.
            Psychiatric help and weight loss is what
            you need.

The girls then continue to laugh, Miranda grabs her bag, cookies
and clothes and runs off the field. She goes to the steps of the
hill that lead to the field and sits. She watches the
cheerleaders do their tryout while she eats cookies.

Serena, Kelsey and Jennie look over and see Miranda watching, they
stop there tryouts and come over. Miranda stands up to leave.

                                               (CONTINUED)

CONTINUED:

                    SERENA:
          Hey, wait, where are you going?

                    MIRANDA:
          Just leaving, next period starts soon.

                    JENNIE:
          Why are you leaving, don't you want to
          stay and watch.

                    MIRANDA:
          Well, I would but I don't think you would
          want me too.

                    SERENA:
          Are you kidding? Why wouldn't we let you
          watch. Is it because of the mean things
          we said back there, listen that's all
          just an act.
          Smoke and mirrors really. Honestly, we
          really like you.

Miranda smiles.

                    MIRANDA:
          Really?

                    SERENA:
          Oh yes, in fact our hearts felt broken
          when you stormed off. Say how about you
          give us some of those delicious cookies
          you brought.

Miranda hands the cookies over, she is all excited and giddy.

                    MIRANDA:
          Oh, I knew you liked me, see its tough
          love they call it. The last time I came
          out you told me I wasn't good enough. I
          went home last night; I did the two-
          finger diet that you suggested and I
          could feel it working. See you see the
          potential in me, but you need to give me
          the facts in order for me to get to where
          I am now. And today in the field I knew
          that you still wanted me to be a part of
          you guys but I still got to work out I
          still got to.....

                                                    (CONTINUED)

CONTINUED:

Mirandas smile fades, she is caught in the middle of her speech.
The girls are leaning their faces over her cookies and with one
loud snort, all three of them spit into her cookies.

                    MIRANDA: (CONT'D)
          .... My, my cookies. Why did you do that
          to my cookies?

                    SERENA:
          Listen dear we don't give a fuck about
          you. I mean how can you be so naive as to
          think my kind would ever be caught dead
          hanging out with your kind. You're the
          very definition of a worthless pile of
          fat greasy shit. If you were my kind,
          you be the mongrel of our group, the pup
          in a newborn litter that the mother
          disowns for being a runt. No, you will
          never be like us.

They throw Miranda's cookies to the ground and stomp all over
them.

                    MIRANDA:
          You lied to me; you never liked me.

                    SERENA:
          Ding ding ding, looks like we have a
          winner. Jennie tell the lady what she's
          won.

                    JENNIE:
          This pile of dog shit.

Jennie is pointing to a pile of shit that a dog had left by the
stairs.

                    SERENA:
          Well shall we give the winner her prize
          then.

The three girls grab Miranda and haul her over to the pile. They
kick her legs until she falls to her knees.

                    MIRANDA:
          Why are you doing this to me? Why are you
          being so mean?

CONTINUED:
                    KELSEY:
          Because were mean girls bitch, it's what
          we do.

                    SERENA:
          Honestly Miranda, you still don't
          understand do you. This is high school
          sweetie, out in the real world your kind
          may thrive over my kind but in here were
          the queens that run this joint. You know
          it's depressing how much you want to be
          friends with us, were so mean and
          hateful yet you come running right back.
          So desperate you even force yourself to
          puke just to fit in, God not even we do
          that. Just except who you are, and we
          can all move one with our lives. This
          way is really a last resort, maybe now
          you'll stay away from us.

                    MIRANDA:
          No, no, no please.

They push her down onto her belly and her face into the shit.
Serena bends down and starts rubbing Mirandas face in it.

                    SERENA:
          Like a dog you must rub their face in
          their shit to teach them to behave.

They walk away leaving Miranda, crying and puking with her face
covered in shit.

                    SERENA: (CONT'D)
          Enjoy your shit and cookies bitch.

INT. SILVERCREEK HIGH HALL - CONTINUOUS.

Stacy has made her way back to the school, she is digging through
her locker taking out her books for her class.
People wander the hallway, groups of kids snickering at her as
she walks by.

They are looking at their phones and Ipads, tablets they all have
opened and appear to be watching the same thing. Kids are
pointing and staring at her. A group of STUDENTS standing close
to her locker are whispering loudly enough that she can overhear
them.

CONTINUED:

                    TEENAGER #1:
          Is that her?

                    TEENAGER #2:
          Ya dude that's the chick from the video.

                    TEENAGER #1:
          I got a camera you think she make a film
          with us?

Some GIRLS walk by her gossiping.

                    GIRL #1:
          There's that whore, you know I hear she
          begged them to film it. Her own personal
          sex tape.

                    GIRL #2:
          Can't believe she would show her face at
          school.

Stacy closes her locker and heads towards the bathroom, trying to
hide her face in shame.

INT.GIRLS BATHROOM - CONTINUOUS

She goes into the first stall and starts to dig out bottles of
pills the ones she had at home and proceeds to pop a few. She
quickly puts the pills back into her pocket when she hears the
door open.

She walks out of the stall to wash her hands off in the sink, the
girls that have come into the bathroom are Serena, Kelsey and
Jennie. They are still wearing their cheerleading uniforms.

                    SERENA:
          Oh, hey girls look it's the queen of the
          movie screen herself. We were just
          talking about you.

                    KELSEY:
          Ya we were, we were just talking about
          what we say when we ran into you.

                    STACY:
          I have nothing to say.

CONTINUED:

                    SERENA:
          That's OK, just listen then. You see we
          were just wondering what led you to
          quit the cheerleading team?

By now they are slowly pushing Stacy up against the wall and
farther away from the door.

                    SERENA:(CONT'D)
          Was it because of that video that's been
          going around. I didn't realize how much
          that hurt you, I just only wanted people
          to see your true talent. Everyone knows
          you're a whore. Taking three guys on at
          once, that's impressive I mean well
          done.

                    STACY:
          Those boys raped me, and you know it.

The girls begin to chuckle.

                    SERENA:
          Oh, we know, I mean you got all the proof
          on that video. But I don't think you're
          going to tell anybody, I mean after all
          there would be an investigation but you
          can't point fingers at who did it. Their
          faces were never seen on camera.

                    STACY:
          It was your boyfriend Mike and his stupid
          friends.

                    JENNIE:
          You hear that, she's admitting to fucking
          your boyfriend.

                    SERENA:
          So she is, see here's the thing Stacy. I
          know who was in those videos, I mean you
          came to my party you were one of us and
          you decided to make out with my
          boyfriend. I wasn't having any of that,
          so I thought up the plan spiked your
          drink and told my boyfriend that for one
          night he was a free man.

                                                  (CONTINUED)

CONTINUED:

Stacy looks shocked, she has a hard time trying to find her words.

                    STACY:
          So...so you, you organized all that. You
          let your boyfriend and his friends rape
          me. Why? We were friends, we grew up
          together.

                    SERENA:
          The missing part is "used to be" we used
          to be friends. Up to that night, we were
          all friends until you kissed my man. And
          to think he was all game for it, only
          condition I had was that they had to film
          it. So, I lent the camera, and Chris
          filmed it, he's a watcher that one is.
          It's a good thing you left the team, we
          don't tolerate boyfriend fuckers.

They push Stacy past them and let her run to the door.

                    SERENA:(CONT'D)
          Just a few words of advice, watch your
          back. My boyfriend is itching to make a
          sequel.

Stacy leaves the bathroom crying but she is stopped in the hall
when she runs into PRINCIPAL PETER GOLDSTEIN (40).

                    PRINCIPAL GOLDSTEIN:
          Stacy, what seems to be the matter?

                    STACY:
          Nothing, everything's fine just having a
          moody day that's all.

                    PRINCIPAL GOLDSTEIN:
          Well let's go into my office and talk
          about it, I think there's something we
          need to discuss.

INT. PRINCIPALS OFFICE - CONTINUOUS.

He leads her into her office, VICE PRINCIPAL CHANDLER GRIEVES
greets Stacy when she first walks through the door.

                    VICE PRINCIPAL GRIEVES:
          Morning Stacy, you're not looking to well
          is everything ok?

CONTINUED:

                    PRINCIPAL GOLDSTEIN:
          She's fine just needs to sit in my office
          and discuss something. Hold all my calls
          till we're done.

                    VICE PRINCIPAL GRIEVES:
          Should I at least get her something to
          drink?

                    PRINCIPAL GOLDSTEIN:
          I said she's fine. Now come this way Mrs.
          Lawrence.

He leads her into his office which is painted a mixture of both
orange and yellow. Filling Cabinets and bookshelves line one side
of the wall. In the center is his desk, he has an old desktop
computer and keyboard sitting on the desk.
There is also another door in the room which leads to the security
room, where they keep all the monitors.

Principal Goldstein sits and motions to the other chair for Stacy
to take her seat. He pulls out a tablet from his desk drawer.

                    PRINCIPAL GOLDSTEIN:
          This came across my desk this morning,
          some youngsters were in the halls playing
          with this when I confiscated it.

                    STACY:
          And what does it have to do with me?

                    PRINCIPAL GOLDSTEIN:
          Well, it contains a very sexually
          explicit video, one of which you are
          the star of.

Stacy reaches for the tablet, but the principal holds it out of
her reach.

                    PRINCIPAL GOLDSTEIN:(CONT'D)
          Now this video has gone viral around
          this campus, I imagine all the students
          have seen it by now and for that I am
          sorry. But when I asked you what the
          matter was why didn't you tell me, this
          is a very serious matter. Police need to
          be involved.

CONTINUED:
                    STACY:
          I don't need the police involved I need
          people to just leave me alone.

                    PRINCIPAL GOLDSTEIN:
          Why? So those boys can get away with it?
          You don't have to be afraid of them, and
          in cases like these if you're feeling
          like it's your fault then trust me when
          I tell you that it's not. I want to help
          you, will you let me do that?

Stacy calms down, she now accepts the offer for help. She nods
her head.

                    STACY:
          Yes, yes, I guess I would like that very
          much.

                    PRINCIPAL GOLDSTEIN:
          Good I'm glad to hear it, cases like
          these are very serious and come at a
          cost.

                    STACY:
          I'm confused. A cost?

Principal Goldstein stands up and positions himself on the front of
his desk inches away from Stacy. His tone is no longer of a man
wanting to help.

                    PRINCIPAL GOLDSTEIN:
          You know I watched that video, the
          things you could do. Woo wee, not even
          my wife knows how to do it. It really
          turned me on you know, seeing you lying
          there on that bed. I figure if you want
          my help, then you're willing to do a
          little something for me.

He starts to unbuckle his belt; Stacy jumps up frightened.

                    STACY:
          You're a monster, you don't want to help
          me at all.

                    PRINCIPAL GOLDSTEIN:
          Ah don't be like that, come on. Do you
          want my help or not?

Stacy storms off out of the office, crying, screaming.

                                                    (CONTINUED)

CONTINUED:

                         STACY:
          You disgusting pig, get away from me.

Principal Goldstein runs after her but stops, she has left. He
turns towards the vice principal who is staring at him, confused.

                         PRINCIPAL GOLDSTEIN:
          What the fuck are you looking at? Get
          back to work.

He walks back into his office and slams the door.

INT.BOYS BATHROOM - SAME.

Blake is taking a piss at the urinal; he is just buttoning up his
pants when Mike and the gang come into the room. It is almost an
entire mimic of the scene between Stacy and Serena, where the
boys force Blake up against the bathroom wall.

                    MIKE:
          Look what we have here boys, a girl in
          the men's bathroom.

                    CHRIS:
          What do you think we should do about
          that?

                    JOHN:
          Dunk his head in the toilet, give him an
          old fashioned swirly.

                    MIKE:
          Boys, let's not be kids here. I say we
          make him take his pants off, show us his
          vagina.

Blake laughs.

                    BLAKE:
          Well then, you're going to be sadly
          disappointed. I'm not a woman I very
          much have a penis.

                    MIKE:
          Oh, do you, cause from what I know you
          like the penis. And only woman and
          faggots like penis, so if you're not a
          woman then your obviously a faggot.

CONTINUED:

                    BLAKE:
          I'm not a faggot!

Mike punches Blake in the gut as hard as he can, causing Blake to
lose his balance.

                    MIKE:
          No, no you're a faggot. I want to hear
          you say it.

                    BLAKE:
          Say what?

                    MIKE:
          Say I'm a faggot.

                    BLAKE:
          You're a faggot.

Mike and his buddies laugh, he punches him harder in the gut.

                    MIKE:
          So, you're a comedian as well huh, got
          any more jokes you like to tell.

                    BLAKE:
          Just one.

Blake reaches for the gun he has hidden in the back of his jeans.
He reaches around to pull it out when the bathroom door opens and
in comes DEREK GRANT, Blake's friend. Blake stops what he's doing
and quickly tucks the gun back in his pants and covers his shirt
over it. Derek hurries over and aids Blake, coming in between him
and the others.

                    DEREK:
          Wow wow wow, hold up. What do you guys
          think you're doing?

                    MIKE:
          Just playing around with your lady friend
          here. He was about to tell us a joke.

                    DEREK:
          Well, it looks like he had enough why
          don't you leave him alone. Save the
          joking for another day.

                                                    (CONTINUED)

CONTINUED:
                         MIKE:
                Ok, fair enough. We'll peace out, you
                still coming over tonight to party?

                         DEREK:
                Man, you know me, I never miss a good
                time.

They walk out of the bathroom, leaving Derek to tend to Blake.

                         DEREK:(CONT'D)
                Man, it's a good thing I came in when I
                did. Boys would have roughed your ass up.

                         BLAKE:
                Thanks, but I think I could have taken
                care of myself.

                         DEREK:
                And it sure looked like it too. Hey man
                if your all right I going to head back
                to class.

                         BLAKE:
                Ya I'm fine.

                         DEREK:
                Great, I'll see you later after class.

Derek goes to leave the bathroom but stops, he's standing with the
door open.

                         DEREK:(CONT'D)
                Hey that picture you got on Facebook, you
                don't mine doing me a favor and taking it
                down would you.

                         BLAKE:
                Why? Don't you like it?

                         DEREK:
                It's a good picture and all, but with
                the heart it really makes the picture
                say something else. And I don't want
                people getting the wrong impression about
                us, it's cool were friends and all but I
                don't want people to start thinking were
                weird or anything.

CONTINUED:

                         BLAKE:
          Weird?

                         DEREK:
          Ya the picture really makes it seem like
          maybe you like me, and I know you're gay
          and all but I mean common were friends
          you honestly don't like me like that do
          you?

Blake looks at him puzzled, almost heartbroken.

                         BLAKE:
          Na man are you kidding me I don't like
          you like that; I can find a man better
          then you. I'll take it down after school.

                         DEREK:
          Alright thanks man.

Derek leaves the bathroom, after a moment Blake heads off to class
too.

INT. HISTORY CLASSROOM - AFTERNOON.

Mike and his gang, and Serena and her groupies are all seated in
the classroom together. They share the same class with Blake,
Brian and Miranda and a few other students.

Mike and the boys are re-watching the video of Stacy and them on
their phones. The volume is turned up so the class can hear the
moaning and groaning of the people on tape.

                         MIKE:
          See this is where the part gets good.

They all start laughing at the video. Blake turns to Mike and the
gang.

                         BLAKE:
          That's honestly disgusting that you sit
          there and watch that gross video. Have
          you no sympathy for her.

                         CHRIS:
          What's the matter, you upset that you
          weren't apart of the video.

CONTINUED:

                    SERENA:
          Maybe me and the girls could make one
          with him.

                    MIKE:
          Na sweetie he's a penis gobbler, he much
          prefers it if it was me and the boys here
          riding his ass off. Would that make you
          feel better?

                    HENRY:
          I don't know why he's so upset about it,
          his mother used to make all kinds of
          videos with the town folk. Do you even
          know who your real dad is?

The class continues to laugh; the teacher MRS.OLIVIA WINTERS is
sitting at the front. She is doing a crossword, paying no attention
to the conversation that is around her.

                    JOHN:
          I wonder if his mother and Brian's mother
          ever made a video.

                    BRIAN:
          Shut the fuck up, my mother is not a
          whore.

                    JOHN:
          You're right I apologize, she's a dead
          whore.

By this time the teacher has become alert to Brian's shouting.

                    MRS.WINTERS:
          Mr. Monroe, if you have another outburst
          like that then I'll be forced to send you
          to the principal's office.

Brian and Blake get up to walk out of the class, they're tired of
all the nonsense.

                    MRS.WINTERS:(CONT'D)
          And just where do you think you're going?
          Class isn't over yet.

                    BRIAN:
          I'm tired of this school and
          everybody's bullshit. I'm going home,
          fuck this.

Brian and Blake storm out of the classroom.

                    Mrs. Winters:

The dynasty, during their rule, would leave their enemies alive,
disfiguring them in a most grotesque manner. It was a message to all
those who would oppose their rule that you would die, or carry the
scars of your defiance. There was a price to pay for your actions. By
the time they were through with you, death would be a welcome friend.

(CONTINUED)

EXT. SILVERCREEK HIGH - CONTINUOUS.

Brian and Blake walk outside to the benches and sit down, Brian is
fuming mad.

                    BRIAN:
          We can't go on being treated like this,
          this school and everyone inside it needs
          to pay.

                    BLAKE:
          I'm with you on that one but I don't see
          how we can do it. Besides we're so close
          to graduation let's just wait it out.

                    BRIAN:
          Na, I can't wait that long. Something
          needs to be done now and fast.

                    MIRANDA:
          What you got in mind?

Miranda has left class and found the boys sitting at the bench, she
is intrigued by their conversation.

                    BLAKE:
          Why do you want to be a part of this?

                    MIRANDA:
          After you left, they resorted to calling
          me fat and ugly. They made fun of me on
          the field today, rubbed my face in shit.

                    BRIAN:
          They humiliated me on the field as well,
          four men tackled me to the ground.

                    MIRANDA:
          I say that didn't realize it was you.

                    BLAKE:
          Your hair, what happened to it?

                    MIRANDA:
          I cut it myself last night, it's hideous
          isn't it.

(CONTINUED)

CONTINUED:

                    BLAKE:
          Oh no, on the contrary I really enjoy it,
          really brings out your inner beauty.

                    MIRANDA:
          Why thank you.

Brian stands up to address them.

                    BRIAN:
          As much as I love this little bonding
          moment we're sharing we need to get back
          to the task at hand.
          What are we going to do about the
          bullies?

Stacy has overheard there little conversation and she approaches
the group.

                    STACY:
          If you want a plan, I think I might have
          something in mind.

INT. BRIAN MONROE'S HOUSE - LIVING ROOM - NIGHT.

Brian sits in his home, flipping through the tv channels when his
dad walks through the door.

                    OFFICER MONROE:
          So how did things go today in the field.
          You make the team?

                    BRIAN:
          No, I didn't, they tossed me around like
          a rag doll.

His father walks over and examines the marks on his face.

                    BRIAN:(CONT'D)
          There is nothing to worry about, just
          battle scars.

                    OFFICER MONROE:
          You and I both know you don't get this
          type of bruise on the field. I mean for
          Christ's sake, you're missing two
          teeth, your eye looks like it's about
          to pop.

CONTINUED:

                    BRIAN:
          It was Mike and his buddies, roughed me
          up in the locker room.

                    OFFICER MONROE:
          And did you tell the coach?

                    BRIAN:
          The coach stood there and watched.

                    OFFICER MONROE:
          Why didn't you call me to come get you,
          do I need to go into the school and have
          a talk with them.

                    BRIAN:
          I don't need you fighting my battles for
          me dad. I can fight my own, even if I get
          my ass kicked. Look at me, I took their
          beating like a champ.

Officer Monroe doesn't look like he fully believes his son, he
gets up and precedes to walk down to the basement and puts away his
gun and baton into the safe. Brian followed.

                    OFFICER MONROE:
          Well promise me you won't go and do
          anything stupid.

                    BRIAN:
          I promise.

                    OFFICER MONROE:
          Good then let's go get something to eat,
          and I'll get an ice pack that thing looks
          nasty.

His father walks upstairs, leaving Brian alone again in the
basement. Brian turns to the safe and turns the dial.
11-23-15. Click. Open. Brian smiles as he gazes at the two
shotguns, he closes the safe.

INT. SCHOOL HALLS - NIGHT.

Someone is walking down the halls after hours; the lights are off
and there is no one else around. The person is wearing gloves as
they slip invitation letters into lockers. The invitations read
"COME CELEBRATE THE PROM KING AND QUEEN."

INT.FARMHOUSE - NIGHT.

Four individuals wake up in a dark room, the lights of the barn
flick on and we notice that each one of them is beside the other,
tied to chairs in a circle. They have bags over their heads and
tape on their mouths, all that can be heard is their mumbling as
they come too.

The sound of footsteps can be heard coming into the room. The
same individual from the school appeared into the room although
we don't see their faces. They take a bag off one of the
individuals heads, then proceed to move on to the next. All four
individuals are Mrs. King, Mrs. Winter, Mr. Simmons and Mr.
Goldstein. The teachers from the school are scared, sweat runs
down their face or is it tears.

The individual rips the tape off Mr. Goldstein's mouth. He holds a
knife to his throat.

                    PRINCIPAL GOLDSTEIN:
          It's you, why why are you doing this. We
          have families, they'll know we're missing
          they'll send help, they're going to come
          looking for us, you won't get away with
          this.
          You'll hang for this you hear me; you'll
          hang.

The individual runs the knife along Mr. Goldstein's face, you can
hear someone shushing him before the blade tears into his face. He
screams, and so does the muffled sound of the others.

INT. SCHOOL CAFETERIA - AFTERNOON.

Blake is sitting alone at the table eating, police are roaming
through the school coming in and out of teachers offices. Derek
sits down at the table beside him.

                    DEREK:
          So, what's the deal with all the police
          around here, big drug bust or something?

                    BLAKE:
          Na man, apparently some of the teachers
          never made it home last night. The
          families got scared and called the
          police, they're in here to investigate.

CONTINUED:

                    DEREK:
          How they know their missing, could be out
          on strike. Teachers not showing up to
          classes and graduation is just around the
          corner. This better not affect me
          getting out of here on time.

                    BLAKE:
          Relax, I'm sure we'll all be up on the
          stage together when the time comes. It's
          just a few missing teachers, we always
          have substitutes.

They laugh and continue their meal, Derek pulls a letter out of his
pocket.

                    DEREK:
          Look I almost forgot, I got this today
          in my locker. It's a party invitation
          for the prom king and queen. Weird though
          that it doesn't say who's hosting it.

Blake snaps the note from Derek's hands.

                    BLAKE:
          Derek promise me you won't go to this
          party.

                    DEREK:
          Hey man chill, what's your problem?

                    BLAKE:
          This party isn't for you, promise me you
          won't go to this party.

                    DEREK:
          Ah I get it, you weren't invited. So,
          you're going to try to convince me not to
          go too is that it.

                    BLAKE:
          I don't give a fuck about getting invited
          just promise me you won't go there.

                    DEREK:
          Wow ok, I promise. If it makes you feel
          better, I won't go then. Jeez.

Derek gets up from the table and leaves, leaving Blake alone to finish his meal. Blake is too pissed off to eat, he scales his tray across the table and onto the floor.

EXT. SILVERCREEK HIGH - CONTINUOUS.

Outside Brian, Miranda and Stacy are sitting on the benches watching as the students go by. Brian is staring at Mike who is talking to a COP.

                    MIRANDA:
          So, you think he will come?

                    BRIAN:
          It's a party in his honor I'm sure he
          will come. The others will gladly follow
          behind.

                    STACY:
          And the cop he's talking to do you think
          he's telling him about the mysterious
          invitations he received.

                    BRIAN:
          It's his party, they'll keep this well-
          hidden I'm sure of it. He doesn't want
          any cops raiding the place, especially if
          it's his dad walking through the door.

Blake comes over, he grabs Brian by the collar of his shirt.

                    BLAKE:
          Which one of you invited Derek to the
          party?

                    BRIAN:
          What are you talking about? Derek who?

                    BLAKE:
          Derek my friend, we agreed he was off
          limits. He isn't like the others.

                    BRIAN:
          Can you let go of me I can assure you
          that it wasn't any of us.

                    BLAKE:
          Then how'd he get an invitation?

                                                    (CONTINUED)

CONTINUED:
                        BRAIN:
          I swear it wasn't us, maybe it got
          dropped into the wrong locker by
          mistake. I can't tell you how it got
          there, because I don't know.

Blake lets go of Brian who begins to adjust his shirt collar.

                        MIRANDA:
          So did you tell him not to come.

                        BLAKE:
          Without it trying to look too
          suspicious and give anything away I'd
          advised him not to come. He promised, I
          think it's safe to say that he won't be.
          Close call though.

                        STACY:
          Let's get down to business then shall we.

They are all grouped around the table now as Stacy begins to go
over the plan.

                        STACY:(CONT'D)
          So, Brian I assume you can get into you
          safe alright and get to those shotguns.

                        BRIAN:
          My dad will be working till 10 but with
          this missing teacher crisis his hands
          will be tied. The cops will be out of
          our hair for the night. So, I can get
          the guns and get them back before my dad
          even knows they are gone, however two of
          you will have to carry them. My week
          frame won't be able to support the weight
          of the gun.

                        BLAKE:
          Me and Miranda will take them, I'll bring
          my six shooter for you for extra
          assurance.

                        MIRANDA:
          And I can take my father's side arm that
          he keeps up in the closet, he never pays
          attention he won't notice it gone.

CONTINUED:

                    STACY:
          Excellent, I've required all the
          necessary tools and equipment we need.
          They are all out at the farm house and
          ready to go.

                    BLAKE:
          And we're sure this place is safe to use.
          Nobody will stumble upon it will they?

                    STACY:
          It's far back in the sticks enough that
          no one even knows it exists.

                    BRIAN:
          And what about the property, who does it
          belong to?

                    STACY:
          Nothing that will be traced back to us.
          Which reminds me, we'll be wearing masks,
          anybody got a problem with that?

The rest shake their heads.

                    MIRANDA:
          What kind of masks did you have in mind?

Stacy pulls out her phone shows a still framed image from the
rape video.

                    STACY:
          Ones identical to these. A sheep, a wolf
          and a rabbit.

                    MIRANDA:
          And the fourth mask?

                    STACY:
          A chicken. The camera man wore a chicken
          mask. I want them to know exactly why
          they are there.

INT. BRIANS BASEMENT - NOON.

Brian is home alone; he quickly grabs the guns and ammunition. He
stares for an extra moment before grabbing the extra bullet proof
vest. He puts it on under his sweater and heads back upstairs. As
he's leaving a letter falls out of

                                                    (CONTINUED)

his back pocket, it's an invitation. He doesn't notice it as it falls to the floor, he goes outside and jumps into a van where Blake awaits.

EXT.FARMHOUSE - CONTINUOUS.

Cars are pulling up the long-twisted path towards the farmhouse. There are no lights on, the place seems to be deserted.

The cars come to a stop and the passengers get out.

Mike with his girlfriend hanging off his arm, the others all hollering and cheering. "Let's get this party started."

                    SERENA:
          Are you sure this is the right place?
          Doesn't seem like theirs much going on.

                    MIKE:
          This is the place babe, there's a party
          for us going on inside.

Serena looks around, the place is surrounded by trees, the sky is barely visible amongst them all. The building itself is in rough shape, it's at least two stories tall, the shutters are bolted shut across the windows. There is no music playing, no lights glowing. There isn't any evidence of a party going on inside. The farm in weathered stained, exposure to rain had caused the wood to soften and break.

                    SERENA:
          I don't know. This place gives me the
          creeps, there isn't any sign of life
          around. It's just us.

                    MIKE:
          Well, the invitation did say the party
          was only for a select few, I guess were
          that select few. Come on, don't you want
          to party.

                    KELSEY:
          Ya Serena's right, if there was supposed
          to be a party then why don't I hear
          anything.

With that being said music begins to play, loud obnoxious dub step music.

CONTINUED:

                    MIKE:
          woo looks like we got us a party.

He grabs his woman by the hands, and they all storm off into the
barn. They pry the door open and step inside, carrying there beer,
kegs and funnels into the barn with them.

Over on the wall written in glow in the dark green paint says,
"Welcome to the party."

The door behind them closes shut and the music stops.

                    CHRIS:
          Hey, I can't get the door open, what's
          going on. Somebody turn on the lights.

The lights come on just as he says that.

                    CHRIS:(CONT'D)
          Who did that?

Everybody shakes their head; they look around confused. In the
front of the room is a punch bowl, plastic cups beside it. There
is also a handwritten note.

                    MIKE:
          Hey guys I guess we got us some drinks
          over here.

Mike picks up the card.

                    SERENA:
          What does it say?

                    MIKE:
          It says "Drink up and let the party
          begin. Your host will be with you
          shortly." Well alright let's see what
          this guy has to offer.

                    SERENA:
          I don't think we should be drinking that;
          we don't even know who our host is yet.

                    MIKE:
          Babe, since when have you ever let that
          stop you from taking a free drink from
          someone you don't know. Lighten up and
          stop being a bitch.

(CONTINUED)

CONTINUED:

Mike hands out the drinks, Serena hesitates but takes a cup from
him. Mike raises the glass out in front to cheer. The rest follows.

                    MIKE:
          Here's to the prom king and queen, let
          the good times roll.

Everyone cheers and downs their drink.

                    JOHN:
          Is it just me or did that taste funny to
          anyone else?

The quick acting drug sets in, they all stumble on their feet.
Mike and Chris make their way to the door.

                    MIKE:
          Guys help us with this door, we need to
          get out. Somethings wrong.

Mike sounds completely incoherent. Like a drunk he falls on his
ass but so do the others. Collapsed in the middle of the floor.
Lights out as they pass out.

INT.FARMHOUSE - NIGHT.

When Mike and the others come to, they are all sitting upright
next to each other. They try to adjust their eyes to their
surrounds.

                    HENRY:
          Dude, what happened?

                    MIKE:
          I don't know, I think we were drugged.

Mike goes to stand up and walk around but trips and falls. He
looks at his ankle, there are cuffs around his foot, with his
ankle being attached to the person sitting next to him, his
girlfriend. Everyone's ankles were shackled and attached to
someone sitting next to them.

                    MIKE:(CONT'D)
          What the fuck is going on?

Everyone is panicking when a voice from above can be heard.
Everyone looks up at the balcony. Standing before them are four
masked figures. A rabbit, sheep, wolf and chicken. All brandishing
guns.

CONTINUED:

                    BRIAN/MR.WOLF:
          This is your party, and we are your
          hosts.

Act 2.1

ACT 2.1

The bullies turned into hostages are sitting together, chained.
They are in constant fear, some of the girls begin to cry. The
farmhouse has long since been vacant, the stalls that would have
kept the animals enclosed have been removed, making more room to
move around in. There are three doors on the main floor, the one
where the group came in, another to the back which also leads
outside and one that leads into another room. A set of stairs to
the front leads to the second floor, most likely where the
farmers at the time had stored hay. It is all bare except for the
four masked individuals standing before them. A breaker to the
side of the wall at the top of the stairs for the lights, the
paint still visible on the side wall. The side doors have chains
wrapped around the handles with a lock.

                    MIKE:
          Who are you? What are you going to do
          with us?

                    BRIAN/MR.WOLF:
          That's a very good question, but a
          better question would be to ask why you
          are here.

Brian and the others descended the stairs, there guns still aimed
at their hostages.

                    KELSEY:
          Why are we here? We've done nothing
          wrong. Who are you people?

Miranda begins to laugh.

                    MIRANDA/MS.SHEEP:
          You cannot be serious. You're here
          because people like you have bullied,
          hurt, tortured people and have gotten
          away with it for far to long. Don't let
          your ignorance cloud your mind, you know
          exactly why you're here.

                    MIKE:
          So, we bullied you, is that it? Look
          we're just kids we don't know any better
          please just leave us alone.

                    BRIAN/MR.WOLF:
          Leave you alone, why so you can go back
          to school tomorrow and do the same shit
          you do every day. No,

                              (MORE)

                                              (CONTINUED)

CONTINUED:

                    BRIAN/MR.WOLF: (cont'd)
          where here to teach you a lesson, to
          know what it feels like to be helpless.
          Where not going to kill you, oh no, but
          the suffering will be far greater than
          you could ever imagine. By tonight you'll
          have wished we did kill you.

They cling to one another, scared they have never been submitted to
someone with higher power over them.

                    SERENA:
          So, tell us then, what are you going to
          do?

                    CHRIS:
          Is this all just a scare tactic, a cruel
          prank to make us amend our ways?

                    BRIAN/MR.WOLF:
          I can assure all of you that this is no
          cruel prank, this is all going to be
          quite...physical.

He points to the objects to the front of the room, where the table
and punch bowl originally had been is now set to the side. There
is now an assortment of tools and traps, a wash bucket, jugs of
water, what appears to be a bag of flour, two burlap sacks filled
with items. The beer and funnels that Mike and the others come in
with are all there as well.

                    BRIAN/MR.WOLF:(CONT'D)
          Shall we get started then.

He walks over a picks up a burlap sack and shakes it in front of
the group.

                    BRIAN/MR.WOLF:(CONT'D)
          While you were all passed out after
          drinking our little concoction, we took
          the liberty of taking your phones and
          car keys and placing them in this here
          bag.

He begins to pour one of the jugs of water into the bag, destroying
their phones. He picks it up and for extra measure, smashes the
bag back and forth off the floor.

                              (MORE)

CONTINUED:

                    BRIAN/MR.WOLF: (CONT'D)
          Didn't want any of you to get the idea of
          calling for help.

                    BLAKE/MR.RABBIT:
          It's funny really how you all sit there,
          wondering why you're here in the first
          place. Honestly you could have all left
          given the chance at the beginning, the
          sketchy letters you received the creepy
          area it was in. You all could have left,
          leaving us here and our plan would have
          failed. But no you're all so goddamn
          pigheaded and arrogant that you were
          completely unaware of the possibly
          danger that you were stepping into. The
          door wasn't even locked we were standing
          outside leaning up against the door, the
          music just from my iPhone and speakers.
          And still when those lights came on and
          you see that drink you couldn't help
          yourself but go over and have a sip. I'm
          glad to see that you care more about
          ruining your livers than saving your own
          lives. You got yourself into this mess.

                    BRIAN/MR.WOLF:
          I think that's enough, it's about time
          we got this show on the road. I guess
          I'll go first.

He walks over to the other burlap sack and takes out a metal rod,
he brings it forth first to Mike.

                    MIKE:
          What is that? What are you going to do to
          me?

                    SERENA:
          Get away from him with that thing!

                    BRIAN/MR.WOLF:
          This is what farmers call a cattle prod,
          its used to set the cow straight if its
          misbehaving.
          Honestly, I don't know what they use it
          on cows for, I just know it hurts like a
          mother fucker. Think of being tasered by
          a cop, your

                    (MORE)

                                                        (CONTINUED)

CONTINUED:

                    BRIAN/MR.WOLF: (cont'd)
          dads a cop right. I'm sure you know what
          I'm talking about, so think of this as one
          of those only worse.
          How much worse, you ask.

Brian pocks the prob into Mikes arm, the shock cause him to bend
over and scream.

                    HENRY:
          What the fuck stop it you're hurting him.

                    BRIAN/MR.WOLF:
          Oh, I can assure you Mr. Rush that it is
          indeed what we are here to do.
          Make you feel broken, beaten down. Like
          those boys you corner in the showers and
          kick the shit out of them.

Brian walks over to Henry and jabs the prob in his face, he falls
back. Burn marks starting to form where him and Mike were hit.

                    BRIAN/MR.WOLF:(CONT'D)
          Have you ever felt beaten down before,
          cornered with nowhere to run. You boys
          plague our school like a sickness, teens
          suicides are caused by people like you.

                    JENNIE:
          Who are you people?

                    BRIAN/MR.WOLF:
          Just a friendly classmate, someone you
          see walk the halls everyday but pay no
          attention or mind to. These boys broke
          me down, beat me into submission.

Brian shocks John this time then Chris shortly after.

                    BRIAN/MR.WOLF:(CONT'D)
          This is what happens when you hunt like a
          pack of animals. You get put down by a
          pack of animals. You know when Ms.
          Chicken here suggested we wear masks to
          conceal our identity I thought to myself
          that it was a tad bit dumb. I mean surely
          people you picked on in school you
          would.
                    (MORE)

CONTINUED:

                    BRIAN/MR.WOLF:(CONT'D) (cont'd)
          still be able to make out their voices
          but no you're so inconsiderate of the
          people around you you never thought once
          about the person you bullied. How they
          talked, I bet you wouldn't even
          recognize our face if you saw them.

                    MIKE:
          So, the masks, why bother wearing them at
          all then?

                    STACY/MS.CHICKEN:
          I think I'd be better off explaining
          that one. You see these masks resemble
          fear, something I'm sure you won't
          forget for a long time. When you walk
          into a crowded place, and you see these
          masks I want you to think of us. But
          second each and every one of you should
          recognize these masks.

They all stared at her stunned, not one knows what the masks
represent.

                    KESELY:
          Why are they supposed to mean something
          to us?

                    CHRIS:
          Honestly were not sure what to think of
          these masks.

Stacy screams out in rage.

                    STACY/MS.CHICKEN:
          You have all got to be fucking shitting
          me. Really you're in this situation and
          your gonna play dumb with me. Maybe this
          will help jog your memory.

She pulls out her phone and loads the video of her being raped. She
holds it out for all of them to see.

                    STACY/MS.CHICKEN:(CONT'D)
          These were the most frightening masks to
          this girl when you held her down and
          raped her. These mark the end of her
          innocent life, the one you stole from
          her. These are.

                    (MORE)

                                              (CONTINUED)

CONTINUED:

                    STACY/MS.CHICKEN:(CONT'D) (cont'd)
          her own personal demons to carry, and
          soon they will be yours as well. You
          know they say when someone is raped it
          feels like dying especially to a women
          and that she goes to this place, this
          realm of dreams like a coma.
          While the perp or perps in this case
          have their way with her. In her dream
          she envisions a normal life, the dream
          expands into eternity; every dream for
          every person is different. Except for one
          thing, something in their head tells them
          that they need to get up, that the attack
          is still going on that she needs to fight
          back and escape. Her mind leaves around
          clues about her condition, it could be a
          letter from an old friend, a text from
          her mother or writing on the walls. It's
          always placed different but it always
          says the same thing, wake up, it's time
          to wake up.

The group look at her stunned, Stacy is crying now as she tells
her story. Even Brian and the others have turned away from the
group. They had never heard this from her, this is her first time
expressing how she felt.

                    SERENA:
          So, you want us to sit here and feel
          sorry for some whore that got raped. I'm
          sorry but I feel no sympathy for trash
          like that.

                    STACY/MS.CHICKEN:
          I don't just want you to feel sorry for
          her, I want you to feel the pain. I want
          you to know what it feels like to want
          to wake up.

                    KELSEY:
          OH MY GOD! You can't be serious you don't
          expect us to do that, do you?

                    SERENA/JENNIE:
          What, what is it?

                    KELSEY:
          Don't you see what this crazy bitch is
          getting at. She wants the boys to rape
          us, make us feel like that tramp in the
          video.

CONTINUED:

                    STACY/MS.CHICKEN:
     Not you...

She points at Serena.

                    STACY/MS.CHICKEN:(CONT'D)
     Her. I want the boys to rape her.

Mike gets back up to his feet.

                    MIKE:
     Don't you dare touch a fucking hair on
     her head you fucking pigs.

With a quick motion, Brian jabs the prod into Mikes side sending
him falling back on his ass.

                    BRIAN/MR.WOLF:
     We're not going to do it. You are. You
     and your friends are going to fuck the
     shit out of precious little girlfriend
     here. And we're all going to watch.

Serena is now standing up.

                    KELSEY:
     Serena, what are you doing?

                    JENNIE:
     Ya Serena sit down.

                    SERENA:
     No, I have a say in this, and I'm
     finally standing up against them. You
     say we're the bullies here yet look at
     you, look at the stuff your doing. You
     sadistic mother fuckers. Trying to force
     a rape to happen.

                    STACY/MS.CHICKEN:
     Isn't that what they did, forced
     themselves onto a girl who didn't have
     the advantage of getting away.

                    SERENA:
     That girl was a slut, she deserved every
     pounding she got. But to stand here and
     call them bad, then to try and force
     them onto me well then, your no better
     then we are. So if you want to shoot me
     then fine go ahead and shoot me, but I am
     not

                         (MORE)

                                        (CONTINUED)

CONTINUED:
                    SERENA: (cont'd) going to
          let those boys on me just because you
          want to make things right for that
          whore.

Brian has had enough; he takes the back end of the prod and
smashes it across Serenas face. Stacy storms off to the other end
of the room. Brian leans down and grab Serena by the hair of the
head, holds up her face, blood pouring from her nose.

                    BRIAN/MR.WOLF:
          You listen here you fucking turd, when
          we say you do something you better
          fucking believe you're going to be doing
          it.

He lets go of her head; she grabs her nose. Kelsey by her side
tends to her wounds.

                    MIRANDA/MS.SHEEP:
          Na, I got a better Idea for her. Save
          her for something else. Make one of the
          other girls be punished.

                    BLAKE/MR.RABBIT:
          How about the boys just do it themselves.

                    MIKE:
          Do what ourselves? You mean sex with each
          other? No way man I'm not gay.

                    BRIAN/MR.WOLF:
          Not you, I think I can make better use of
          you. No someone else, someone like these
          two.

He points to John and Henry, who stare at each other in disgust.

                    JOHN:
          No man, nope not going to happen.

                    HENRY:
          Like Mike said, were not gay.

                    BLAKE/MR.RABBIT:
          I don't think you have to be gay at all to
          do this. I mean, it's just to men fucking
          to survive isn't it.
          What's so gay about that?

CONTINUED:

                    JOHN:
          Cause it's two men that's why it's gay.
          Besides why don't you pick someone else,
          how about Chris pick him instead of me.

                    CHRIS:
          Dude, you're selling me up river. Why
          didn't you say you didn't want any of
          this to happen. Why did you have to go
          and bring me into this?

                    JOHN:
          I don't want this to happen, but if it were
          to, I'd rather it be you and him and not
          me.

Blake is laughing at the boys bickering.

                    BLAKE/MR.RABBIT:
          Honestly its cute how you two are
          fighting over who's going to be fucking.
          I've made my choice, and it's John and
          Henry. Besides, we all know Chris is a
          watcher.

                    HENRY:
          Nope I'm with Serena on this one, I'm
          not doing it so you might as well kill
          me. Frankly I was set on the raping her
          part.

                    SERENA:
          Ewe you sick perv, why don't you two just
          fuck and get it over with save all our
          asses.

                    HENRY:
          But mine won't be saved, I am not no
          queer. Besides you got the pretty parts,
          just lie there and take it for a while.

                    MIKE:
          Back off man, that's my woman you're
          talking to.

                    HENRY:
          You know, you say she's yours but I
          can't see a single person in this room
          that she didn't fuck.

CONTINUED:
                    MIKE:
          I said back off.

                    HENRY:
          Or what? You going to come after me,
          were all fucking chained together good
          luck getting over here. You know I think
          the only reason she wanted us to film
          that was because secretly she wanted to
          be in that same position.

Mike slowly climbs back to his feet, but Brain shocks him back
down. He looks at Henry, and he takes the hint to sit down quietly.

                    BRIAN/MR.WOLF:
          Now as much as I enjoy this dispute
          between the two of you, I think both of
          you can wait till later.
          Right now, we have more important things
          at hand. Ms. Sheep, bring me the pills
          will you.

She walks over to the sack and pulls out a medicine bag, she
takes out a yellow bottle of pills and brings them to Brian. He
dumps two into his hand.

                    BRIAN/MR.WOLF:(CONT'D)
          Now I know it's your first time and all,
          and first times can make a boy nervous.
          Almost to the point that he can't even
          achieve an erection. So, to ensure that
          you do what Mr. Rabbit commands of I am
          going to give you each one Viagra to
          help you with your little problem.

He hands one pill each to John and Henry.

                    JOHN:
          We're not doing this, we said we won't.

                    MIRANDA/MS.SHEEP:
          If you don't do this, then we'll be forced
          to cut off all four of your dicks. So,
          what's it going to be?

                    MIKE:
          I'm not losing my dick because of you
          two, just go in there and do it already.

CONTINUED:

                    HENRY:
          We're not doing some broke back
          mountain shit, all of this is out of the
          question.

                    BLAKE/MR.RABBIT:
          Look at how scared they are, so afraid
          that they might turn gay? What is it
          with you and gays? You make fun of them
          because you don't understand them,
          nobody does. You know what this could be
          fun, one of you might find something out
          about himself that he didn't know before.

                    HENRY:
          So, you're going to make us do this.
          Right here in front of everyone.

                    BLAKE/MR.RABBIT:
          No, I'm going to make you go upstairs,
          give you some privacy.

Blake takes out his phone.

                    HENRY:
          And what are you going to do with that?

                    BLAKE/MR.RABBIT:
          I heard you like movies and I thought
          wouldn't it be fun if you guys made
          another one. Gosh I never thought I would
          get to direct anything before.

                    JOHN:
          What are you going to be there?

                    BRIAN/MR.WOLF:
          Both Mr. Rabbit and Ms. Sheep will be
          there to make sure that you perform up to
          par.

He hands Miranda his prod.

                    BRIAN/MR.WOLF:(CONT'D)
          If you feel like you can't do it, Ms.
          Sheep here will be more then gladly zap
          you in the ass until you do so.

CONTINUED:

Brian bends down and unlocks both John and Henrys cuffs. He makes
Jennie sit closer to Chris and cuffs her back with the rest of the
group. John and Henry walk up the stairs with Blake and Miranda
following close behind with their guns pointed.

                    BLAKE/MR.RABBIT:
          Woo lets go make a movie.

Brain looks at the rest of the group.

                    BRIAN/MR.WOLF:
          Now don't go trying anything stupid while
          I'm gone.

INT.BACK END OF FARMHOUSE - CONTINUOUS.

Stacy is sitting by the back door, her hands under her mask rubbing
her eyes. Brian walks up and sits down beside her.

                    BRIAN/MR.WOLF:
          So, we choose the two boys John and Henry
          to do the deed.

                    STACY/MS.CHICKEN:
          Just the two of them?

                    BRIAN/MR.WOLF:
          It was Blakes idea, he wanted them to do
          it to get back at what they did to you.
          It's also fitting seeing as this counts
          as Blakes punishment to towards them.

                    STACY/MS.CHICKEN:
          And serena? What are we going to do with
          her?

                    BRIAN/MR.WOLF:
          I think Miranda has something in mind for
          her and her friends.

Stacy quits rubbing her eyes.

                    STACY/MS.CHICKEN:
          Ya friends. It's funny how I used to be a
          part of that group. Strange to think that
          if they hadn't had done what they done
          that I could still be one of those girls.
          Probably chained up right next to them.

CONTINUED:

                    BRIAN/MR.WOLF:
          You were the one with the idea, it's
          awful to say but if they hadn't had done
          what they done none of this here would
          have happened.
          Miranda probably would have killed
          herself, to tell you the truth I might
          have done the same. And Blake, well he's
          got enough to deal with at home and at
          school that he probably would have shot
          the place up. I think the only person
          keeping him sane is Derek to be honest.

She looks at him, gazing into his eyes.

                    STACY/MS.CHICKEN:
          Do you agree with those girls? Do you
          think I'm a whore?

                    BRIAN/MR.WOLF:
          How could you say such a thing, you're
          not a whore. What those boys did to you
          they could have done to anyone else, you
          were just in the wrong place at the
          wrong time.
          Those boys are monsters, how dare you
          think what they did to you was your
          fault. Do you really think that?

                    STACY/MS.CHICKEN:
          Think what?

                    BRIAN/MR.WOLF:
          That it's your fault.

                    STACY/MS.CHICKEN:
          Sometimes, I look back at it and think
          about all the things I could have
          changed that could have prevented it
          from happening. If I hadn't had gone to
          the party, if I hadn't drunk, if I hadn't
          had tried to kiss Mike, if I hadn't had
          been friends with them. Honestly, I'm
          starting to believe what they say about
          me.

Brian wraps his arm around the back of her neck and pulls her in
close.

CONTINUED:
                    BRIAN/MR.WOLF:
          It's not true and don't you dare think
          about anything else. You're a special
          kind of girl that any man would be glad
          to have, I don't understand why you even
          hung out with them you're not even like
          them.

                    STACY/MS.CHICKEN:
          My mother put me into pageants ever since
          I was little. That's how I met the girls,
          from then on, my mother put me into
          everything. I grew bored of them
          quickly, but my mom didn't I think they
          were more for her anyway then they were
          for me. I grew up and she put me into
          gymnastics then cheerleading. I stuck
          with those girls because they were the
          only people I knew growing up.

                    BRIAN/MR.WOLF:
          Ah so it's your moms fault I get it. Didn't
          you ever tell her you wanted to stop.

                    STACY/MS.CHICKEN:
          I did at first, but I saw the tears in
          her eyes when I told her. So, I stayed
          with it, I guess deep down I always
          wanted to make my mom proud.

Brain lets her lay her head on his shoulder, her then lays his
head on hers.

                    BRIAN/MR.WOLF:
          I know that feeling. I always wanted to
          fit in, to be a part of something. My
          mom died when I was 11, dad was so
          protective of me. Wouldn't let me do
          anything. The first time I didn't make
          the football team he seemed to be so
          relieved about it. But I was crushed,
          all I ever wanted was to make something
          of myself so my mom could be proud. I
          guess bad things happen when people try
          too hard to make their parents happy.

They go silent for a moment.

CONTINUED:

                    STACY/MS.CHICKEN:
          I wish I had the chance to get to know
          you sooner.

                    BRIAN/MR.WOLF:
          You can still get to know me now.

                    STACY/MS.CHICKEN:
          Did I ever make fun of you through
          school.

                    BRIAN/MR.WOLF:
          No, you were one of the cute girls that
          people knew she wasn't with the right
          crowd. You dressed like them but never
          spoke or behaved like them.

Stacy gets back up with her gun and goes to walk over where the
others are.

                    STACY/MS.CHICKEN:
          Thanks. We should be heading back. I
          imagine those boys are done by now
          probably should get a move on with the
          next task.

                    BRIAN/MR.WOLF:
          Do you feel right about all of this?
          About what we're doing?

                    STACY/MS.CHICKEN:
          No, I don't, none of this is right.

                    BRIAN/MR.WOLF:
          I feel like we're getting lost on our
          own path. I don't think this will lead
          anywhere good.

                    STACY/MS.CHICKEN:
          There's a demon inside all of us, an urge
          that drives us forwards.

                    BRIAN/MR.WOLF:
          And how do we kill the demon?

                    STACY/MS.CHICKEN:
          How do you kill a demon inside you,
          without killing yourself.

Brain stands up and goes to go walk with her, but grabs her arm
and stops her.

                                            (CONTINUED)

CONTINUED:

                    BRIAN/MR.WOLF:
          Is it true what you said back there about
          the dream? Did you really slip into a
          dream reality?

                    STACY/MS.CHICKEN:
          No, I lied, there was no dream. God
          didn't want me to sleep that night.

As soon as she is done speaking there is a knock almost like
something is being kicked over. The sound is coming from the room
beside them.

                    BRIAN/MR.WOLF:
          What the fuck was that?

They both go over and open the door to peer inside, he flicks a
light switch on on the side of the wall. They stand there in the
doorway, lifting there masks up to catch the air there so quickly
breathing in.

                    STACY/MS.CHICKEN:
          Well, this can't be good.

INT. BRIANS HOUSE KITCHEN - SAME.

Officer Monroe has come home from work early, he set his jacket
on the table and goes to the living room, he calls out to Brian.

                    OFFICER MONROE:
          Hey Brian, you home, I got off work early
          to grab a bite to eat just wanted to
          check in on you. Where still searching
          for your missing teachers but there
          hasn't been a sign of them for miles.
          Gonna be around your school for another
          couple of days, questioning students.

He waits for a response.

                    OFFICER MONROE:(CONT'D)
          Brian? Brian, you home.

He walks down to Brians room and opens the door.

                    OFFICER MONROE:(CONT'D)
          Brian didn't you just hear me...call for
          you.

CONTINUED:

The room is empty. Officer Monroe walks up to the kitchen again
when he stops and bends down to pick the letter off the floor.

                    OFFICER MONROE:(CONT'D)
               Looks like Brian got himself invited to a
               party. Good for him, it's about time he
               started going out and making friends.

He folds the letter up and puts it in his pocket, he proceeds to
open the fridge and make himself a sandwich.

INT.FARMHOUSE - CONTINUOUS.

Brian and Stacy ran back over to the others, their masks now back
down over their faces. Brian yells up to the others above.

                    BRIAN/MR.WOLF:
               Guys get down here we got ourselves a bit
               of a situation.

Blake peers down over the railing.

                    BLAKE/MR.RABBIT:
               What is it?

                    BRIAN/MR.WOLF:
               Just get down here now, bring the two
               lovers down as well. Chain them up with
               the rest.

Blake nods and disappears back over the railing, after a moment
John and Henry can be seen descending the stairs. The are just in
their boxers, there arms crossed holding themselves. Their eyes
look distant, almost lost within themselves. Neither makes eye
contact with the other. Blake and Miranda are following close
behind, guys aimed.

                    BRIAN/MR.WOLF:(CONT'D)
               Separate the two, give them some space, I
               imagine after the ordeal they won't want
               to be near each other again.

Blake chains John next to Mike, while Miranda chains Henry back
next to Jennie. The order is as follows: John, Mike, Serena,
Kelsey, Chris, Jennie and Henry.

Mike tries to shake John so that he comes aware of his surroundings

                                                      (CONTINUED)

CONTINUED:

                    MIKE:
          Are you ok? Did they make you guys...do
          it?

John shoves Mike away.

                    JOHN:
          I'm fine. I don't want to talk about it,
          just leave me alone.

                    MIKE:
          Are you done here? You've had your fun
          and games you got your payback, now let
          us go.

                    BRIAN/MR.WOLF:
          Oh, we're far from over with. Each one
          of us that stands before you have been
          hurt by you in some way, once we are
          satisfied with how much you have suffered
          then we will let you go.

Blake pulls his phone back out and hits play, both John and Henry
can be heard in the video.

                    BLAKE/MR.RABBIT:
          I think our movie stars have suffered
          enough, don't you think, come Monday
          morning they'll be famous. Everybody will
          have a copy by then.

                    HENRY:
          Please don't send that video out, just
          don't.

Stacy gets down in his face this time, prying his head up so she
can look into his eyes.

                    STACY/MS.CHICKEN:
          And why shouldn't we, after all there
          was no thinking when you released your
          little video the first time. Tell me how
          it felt up there, to be submitted into a
          position you didn't want to be in. Were
          you scared; did you wish for it to stop?

Henry doesn't answer.

CONTINUED:

                    STACY/MS.CHICKEN:(CONT'D)
          Really no response. I was really hoping
          you share with us your experience. Well
          then if you're going to stay quite I
          suggest you keep your fucking mouth shout
          for the rest of the evening.

She stands up and walks away from him.

                    BRIAN/MR.WOLF:
          That goes for the rest of you, we have
          matters to attend to and if you don't
          want your tongues cut out, you'll stay
          quiet till we get back.

INT.BACK END OF FARMHOUSE - CONTINUOUS.

Brian and the rest walk to the back of the barn, they stop by the
door.

                    BLAKE/MR.RABBIT:
          So, the situation you spoke of what is
          it?

                    BRIAN/MR.WOLF:
          Not just one situation to be honest, but
          four.

He opens the door and lying on the floor are four individuals tied
up, hands behind their back. Their heads all have black bags over
them. The room they are in is dimly lit, lots of counters but
mostly barren. It is a room that a farmer would have used to store
his tools and equipment.

                    MIRANDA/MS.SHEEP:
          Who are they?

                    BRIAN/MR.WOLF:
          We don't know. Me and Stacy just found
          them in here like this.

                    BLAKE/MR.RABBIT:
          Well, I guess we should get to the bottom
          of this.

He rips off the mask of the person closest to him, he jumps back
as soon as he sees the person's face. Staring back at them is a
frightened Principal Goldstein. Tape bounds across his mouth. His
nose is broken, eyes are blackened. He mumbles something at them.

                                                    (CONTINUED)

CONTINUED:
                    BLAKE/MR.RABBIT:(CONT'D)
          It's the missing teachers.

                    STACY/MS.CHICKEN:
          How the fuck did they get in here?

They each look at each other, there is a slight bit of distrust
in their eyes.

                    BRIAN/MR.WOLF:
          Ok so this solves the missing teacher
          case but how did they get here? Who
          brought them here?

                    MIRANDA/MS.SHEEP:
          Wasn't any of us? Could someone else be
          using this place too?

                    BRIAN/MR.WOLF:
          Stacy, this place how did you hear about
          this place?

                    STACY/MS.CHICKEN:
          From a friend, someone who prefers to
          remain anonymous. They won't be bothering
          us.

                    BRIAN/MR.WOLF:
          Tell us who this friend is? They might be
          the ones behind this.

                    STACY/MS.CHICKEN:
          I told them that I wouldn't say anything.

                    BLAKE/MR.RABBIT:
          Jesus Christ Stacy, not going to say
          anything. They know about this place;
          did you tell them what we were up to? is
          that why the teachers are here.

                    STACY/MS.CHICKEN:
          I don't know why the teachers are here,
          and I didn't tell anybody about our
          plan.

                    MIRANDA/MS.SHEEP:
          I got a bad feeling about this.

                    BLAKE/MR.RABBIT:
          A bad feeling, of course you got a bad
          feeling. Shit like this gives people bad
          feelings.

CONTINUED:

Pointing to Stacy.

                    BLAKE/MR.RABBIT:(CONT'D)
          You know something and you're not
          telling us. I warn you I'm not going
          down for this. This was supposed to be
          an in and out operation, if we get caught
          it's on you.

Brian pushes him away from her, stepping in between the two of
them.

                    BRIAN/MR.WOLF:
          Back off will you. If she says she
          doesn't know anything or didn't say
          anything, then I believe her. Let's just
          get back to the matter at hand.

                    MIRANDA/MS.SHEEP:
          And what do we do about them, they were a
          big problem in our school too. Should we
          bring them out to join?

                    BRIAN/MR.WOLF:
          No, we leave them here, to many people
          to deal with and not enough chains,
          better off if we just leave them tied up.

Blake puts the black bag down over the principals head and shuts
the door.

INT.FRONT END OF FARMHOUSE - CONTINUOUS.

Mike is getting fed up with this, stands back up and motions to the
others to do the same.

                    MIKE:
          Come on guys, stand up. I'm getting sick
          and tired of sitting around and waiting
          for them to come back and torture us.

                    JOHN:
          And what do you have in mind? If you
          haven't noticed all the doors are locked.

                                                      (CONTINUED)

CONTINUED:

                    MIKE:
          If we all stand together and use our
          force to push up against that we should
          be able to break it down. This place is
          old, doesn't look to sturdy enough force
          and we might be home free.

                    KELSEY:
          Then what once we're outside, where do we
          go. Were all chained together, its gonna
          make running a bitch.

Serena now stands up with her boyfriend.

                    SERENA:
          I'm with Mike on this one, if we all
          work together, we can make it out of
          here. If we just sit here, we will surely
          die.

The others groan but they too stand up, they quickly make their
way to the door. At once all seven of them begin to push.

                    MIKE:
          You hear that, I think it's breaking.
          Come on guys just a little more.

Brian and the others have just finished their conversation at the
back of the room when they notice Mike and his group pushing up
against the door. Brian pulls his gun out of the back of his
pants.

                    BRIAN/MR.WOLF:
          What the fuck do you all think you're
          doing?

Mike and the others turn around slowly.

                    BRIAN/MR.WOLF:(CONT'D)
          Sit the fuck back down before I decide to
          shoot one of you.

                    MIKE:
          Do you even know how to use one of those?

Brian aims the gun into the air and fires. They jump back startled.

CONTINUED:

                    BRIAN/MR.WOLF:
          Does that answer your question. Now sit
          with your asses back on the floor.

They move back into position and sit.

                    BRIAN/MR.WOLF:(CONT'D)
          I think it's time we played a little game
          of which one would you pick.
          Since this is my little game, I'll go
          first.

He walks over and pulls out a bear trap from the front of the
room. He places it in front of Mike and readies the device.

                    BRIAN/MR.WOLF:(CONT'D)
          This is a 40-pound standard bear trap.
          The pressure it gives off when it snaps
          is enough to break a man's leg. So, this
          is what I want you to do. Would you
          rather stick your hand in the trap, or
          would you pick option two which is to cut
          a gash into your girlfriends face.

                    MIKE:
          You can't be serious, this is insane.

Brian laughs.

                    BRIAN/MR.WOLF:
          I've thought we already established that
          everything we were going to do tonight
          was insane. Clearly that first bit
          wasn't crazy enough for you.

                    BLAKE/MR.RABBIT:
          So, what you going to choose, the trap or
          your girlfriend.

Mike turns to his girlfriend; she gasps and slaps him across the
face.

                    SERENA:
          You can't be serious, you're actually
          thinking about cutting me.

                    MIKE:
          It's a little cut, what harm will it do
          you. If I stick my hand in that

                    (MORE)

                                              (CONTINUED)

CONTINUED:

                    MIKE: (cont'd)
          thing it'll surely break, I'll be out of
          football season till I heal.

                    SERENA:
          So, your picking football over your
          girlfriend is that it.

                    MIKE:
          Come on babe just a little cut.

                    SERENA:
          No, you're not cutting me.

                    BRIAN/MR.WOLF:
          So have you made your decision yet.

                    MIKE:
          I choose the trap.

                    BRIAN/MR.WOLF:
          Well good choice then. Now how about we
          get to it shall we.

Mike places his left hand over the trap, he starts to put it in but
quickly hauls it back.

                    BRIAN/MR.WOLF:(CONT'D)
          Now you must do it, those are the rules
          of the game. This is your choice and it's
          final.

                    CHRIS:
          Just put your hand in but quickly draw it
          back out, maybe you can get it out fast
          enough before it goes off.

                    SERENA:
          Just in and out, you can do it.

                    MIKE:
          What if I get my hand in and out and the
          trap doesn't go off. Do I have to do it
          again.

                    BRIAN/MR.WOLF:
          God heavens no, what do you think I am
          some sort of monster. No if the trap
          doesn't go off then we call it survivors
          luck, I guess.

CONTINUED:

Mike takes slow deep breaths to muster up his strength and
courage. He clenches the fingers on his hand back and forth. He
places the hand over the trap.

                    MIKE:
          Ok I can do this.

He lowers his hand onto the pressure plate until his fingers
touch. There is a moment, the fingers touch but the trap doesn't
go off. Mike and the others sigh in relief, then snap. The trap
closes on Mikes hand, everyone gasps.
Chris pukes, Serena puts her hand over her mouth in shock. Mike
just stares and his hand, stunned. Then he starts screaming.

                    MIKE:(CONT'D)
          Get this fucking thing off my hand.

His hand is turning purple, blood pouring out and the bone in his
hand snapped and has torn through skin. He's screaming and crying;
John and Serena pry the trap open enough for him to slip his hand
out of. Mike falls back, clenching his wrist.

                    BRIAN/MR.WOLF:
          Woo that was more fun than I had
          expected.

He takes the trap and scales it to the other side of the room. He
then proceeds to pull a knife out of his pocket. Mike looks up at
him.

                    MIKE:
          What do you think you're doing with that?

                    BRIAN/MR.WOLF:
          Oh nothing, just showing you what you
          could have done.

Brian grabs Serena by the hair of the head, she screams and tries
to get free. Brian takes the open knife and slides it up across
her face. Blood gushing down her cheek.

                    MIKE:
          What the fuck did you do that for? You
          said I had a choice, either I do one or
          the other.

                    BRIAN/MR.WOLF:
          I said you had a choice to do one or the
          other, and you did. I didn't say anything
          about me still not

                    (MORE)

                                              (CONTINUED)

CONTINUED:

                    BRIAN/MR.WOLF: (cont'd)
          cutting her face. You see this situation
          you're in you fail to realize that we're
          in charge here, what we say goes. I told
          you I would make you suffer, to feel
          broken like you made me. Whether
          physically or emotionally was up to you.
          I guess you like to be physical, maybe
          next time you'll think before you decide
          to try and break out again.

Brian places the knife back in his pocket. Miranda steps forth.

                    MIRANDA/MS.SHEEP:
          I guess it is my turn now.

She walks over and from out of the burlap sack she pulls out two
concealed Tupperware containers. She lays them out in front of
both Kelsey and Serena.

                    MIRANDA/MS.SHEEP:(CONT'D)
          Now without peeking, I want you two to
          both pick a container doesn't matter
          which just both of you take one of them.

Serena and Kelsey look at the containers and decide to switch
them.

                    MIRANDA/MS.SHEEP:(CONT'D)
          Oh, being clever are we. Well then have
          it your way. Now I want you to open your
          containers.

They both do. Kelsey had chosen a box filled with dog shit, Serena
however picked a box filled with lipstick and makeup.

                    KELSEY:
          And what are we supposed to do with this.

                    MIRANDA/MS.SHEEP:
          Well, I expect you to eat it.

                    SERENA:
          You expect us to eat makeup and shit.

CONTINUED:
                    MIRANDA/MS.SHEEP:
          Only eat whatever is in the box that you
          choose.

                    KELSEY:
          That's disgusting, I'm not eating dog
          poop.

                    MIRANDA/MS.SHEEP:
          I can assure you it doesn't taste good at
          all. Quite literally you got the shitty
          end of the deal, should have kept the
          one I had placed in front for you.

Serena shoves the container away from her.

                    SERENA:
          We're not eating this, there's no way in
          hell were eating this.

                    MIRANDA/MS.SHEEP:
          Again, with the 'were not doing this'
          crap. By now you should realize the
          predicament you are in. Just think we're
          almost though with your torment, you do
          this and your home free.

Mike is still lying on the floor; he seems to be drifting in and
out of consciousness.

                    MIKE:
          Just do this babe, we've all had our
          share of misfortune tonight. Just do this
          and be down with it.

                    STACY/MS.CHICKEN:
          Ya Serena, listen to what he has to say.
          Just do it and be done with it. No more
          harm will befall you tonight.

                    MIRANDA/MS.SHEEP:
          Well, there's one more thing. Since
          Kelsey here has to eat shit, then I think
          it's only far if we give Serena at least
          one more thing to do.

She grabs one of the tin washtubs and fills it with a bucket of
water. She then dumps in some of what looks like flour into the
water.

CONTINUED:

                    MIRANDA/MS.SHEEP:(CONT'D)
          In addition to your punishment, you must
          also have your face washed with this
          liquid.

                    SERENA:
          What's in the water?

                    MIRANDA/MS.SHEEP:
          Doesn't matter because I'll be applying
          the liquid to your face personally
          myself.

                    BRIAN/MR.WOLF:
          Enough chitchat ladies your burning
          daylight, the sooner you get this done
          the sooner we can all leave, and you can
          get medical attention.

                    MIRANDA/MS.SHEEP:
          Dig in ladies I do hope you enjoy it.

Neither lady wants to do it, they refuse to.

                    MIRANDA/MS.SHEEP:(CONT'D)
          I think they need a little help in doing
          so.

Miranda walks to Kelsey first, taking a big hand full of the shit
out of the container Miranda stuffs it into Kelsey's mouth.

                    MIRANDA/MS.SHEEP:(CONT'D)
          Open wide, here comes the gravy train. Ya
          there you go, doesn't that taste so good.
          Acting like a dog you get treated like
          one.

She continues to stuff the shit into her mouth, Kelsey begins to
cough, tears in her eyes.

                    MIRANDA/MS.SHEEP:(CONT'D)
          Does it really taste that bad. Here, let
          me plug your nose for you while you chew,
          I here that helps when you're eating
          something gross.

Miranda plugs Kelsey's nose, she begins to choke and soon pukes
up the shit as she gasps for air.

                                                        (CONTINUED)

CONTINUED:

                    MIRANDA/MS.SHEEP:(CONT'D)
          Oh well, maybe next time you'll
          appreciate someone's cooking when they
          offer you something.

She turns to Serena.

                    MIRANDA/MS.SHEEP:(CONT'D)
          Do you need help too?

Serena shakes her head and begins to break off piece after piece
of lipstick and she places them into her mouth chewing down on
them. She chokes and coughs and dry heaves a few times but she
manages to get them down.

                    MIRANDA/MS.SHEEP:(CONT'D)
          Does it taste good? Bet you never
          imagined what the stuff you cover you
          whore face in tastes like. Do you feel
          prettier on the inside, has it lightened
          your heart up any? Or is it still as
          black as ever?

                    SERENA:
          I did it, I finished it. Bring on the
          water bitch, they aren't nothing you can
          do that will hurt me.

                    MIRANDA/MS.SHEEP:
          We'll see won't we.

Miranda picks up the tub of water and places it in front of Serena.

                    MIRANDA/MS.SHEEP:
          Let's wash some of that dirty skank off
          your face. Plug your nose, this might burn
          a little.

She hauls onto the top of Serenas head and pushes down, dunking
her face into the water. She holds her head in there for a few
seconds then let's go. Serena brings her head back up, her face is
turning bright red.

                    SERENA:
          What the fuck did you put in that water.
          It burns, on my god its burning me.

Serena digs at her face; the bright redness is quickly turning to
blisters and welts.

CONTINUED:

                    MIRANDA/MS.SHEEP:
          It's a chemical known as lye, what you
          are experiencing is a sever chemical
          burn. Your face will burn and blister,
          you'll be scared for life. To hideous to
          walk in public, people will boo you when
          you are out on the field. Nobody will
          want to be near you, you won't be
          beautiful anymore. So, you see I can
          hurt you, I just took away the one thing
          you hold dearest to you the most. Your
          beauty.

Serena is rolling around on the floor, tearing at the blisters on
her face which are swelling up and busting ooze. She has been
completely disfigured. Miranda walks over and grabs another jug of
water and dumps it on Serenas face as she lays down.

               MIRANDA/MS.SHEEP:(CONT'D)
          You look hideous enough, that should
          stop the burning.

                    BRIAN/MR.WOLF:
          Now there's just one more thing we need
          to take care of. The watcher.

Him and Stacy walk over to Chris, they lean over him one on each
side.

                    CHRIS:
          What ae you going to do with me?

                 STACY/MS.CHICKEN:
          Something simple really.

She takes out a tear dropper, Chris stares at it.

                    CHRIS:
          What are you going to do, cure me of pink
          eye.

                 STACY/MS.CHICKEN:
          No, this here is actually a compound,
          made with the same chemicals we just used
          on your friend over there.

Brian who is standing behind him, gets a firm grasp around his
head and tilts it back.

                                                  (CONTINUED)

CONTINUED:

                    STACY/MS.CHICKEN:(CONT'D)
          We're not curing you of pink eye, were
          curing you of your sight. No more
          watching for the watcher.

She drips the liquid into his eyes, he screams and curses. They
leave him there to suffer, rubbing his eyes red as they begin to
blister and swell up.

They walk up to Jennie, the only one in the group not to get hurt.

                    JENNIE:
          Please, please just do whatever it is and
          get it over with.

                    BRIAN/MR.WOLF:
          We're not going to hurt you, quite the
          opposite. We're letting you go?

They undo her chains and cuff Henry back to Chris.

                    JENNIE:
          Why are you doing this? Why are you
          letting me go?

                    STACY/MS.CHICKEN:
          Well, someone must go and get help for
          their friends. We're not doing it, and
          since you are the only one able to walk
          around unscathed, we volunteer you to
          go.

                    BRIAN/MR.WOLF:
          Just take the path to the road and go
          for help, when you come back your friends
          will still be here, and we will be gone.

                    JENNIE:
          So, you're just letting me go.

                    MIRANDA/MS.SHEEP:
          You could stay it's up to you, I could
          always find something to go with you.

Brian goes over and unlocks the door, without hesitation Jennie
runs off outside which is now getting dark out. Brian shuts the
door but leaves it unlocked. He turns to Blake.

                                                      (CONTINUED)

CONTINUED:

                    BRIAN/MR.WOLF:
          Give her a few second head start then go
          and hurt her down.

                    BLAKE/MR.RABBIT:
          Will do.

Blake with his shotgun walks outside into the night and proceeds to
walk down the trail.

The others sitting on the floor are crying and sobbing, Kelsey
has puked all over herself, Serenas face has become deformed.
Mike lies on the floor unconscious while John and Henry are
sitting in their own little worlds and Chris's eyes have begun to
bleed wither from him tearing at them or from the lye.

John leans over to Mike who isn't moving. He tries to shake him
awake.

                    JOHN:
          Hey, I don't think you guys know this,
          but Mike isn't breathing.

                    BRIAN/MR.WOLF:
          What do you mean he's not breathing?

                    JOHN:
          I mean he must have gone into shock and
          stopped breathing. You have got to do
          something.

                    BRIAN/MR.WOLF:
          We're not here to help you.

                    JOHN:
          But you said you weren't going to kill
          us, if Mike dies then that makes you all
          killers.

                    MIRANDA/MS.SHEEP:
          You have to go do something; he can't die
          we made a promise we wouldn't kill any
          of them.

Brian walks over to Mike and leans down beside him; He presses
his ear against Mikes face to check for any air intake. Mike
opens his eyes and brings his head up, smashing his head into
Brians. Brian stumbles backwards but not before Mike can grab the
gun from out of hand. Mike aims the gun at them, Miranda and Stacy
already have there's pointed at him.

CONTINUED:
                    MIKE:
          No are you going to let us all go or am I
          going to have to shoot one of you.

                    MIRANDA/MS.SHEEP:
          We both got guns too, we'll have you down
          before you even get a shot off.

                    MIKE:
          I can take two of you out before you guys
          bring me down. So, what's it going to be,
          you going to let us go or do you want to
          die.

EXT.PATH TO FARMHOUSE - CONTINUOUS.

Derek is driving in his car up a twisted path, his stereo is
playing rap music and he is singing along.

                    DEREK:
          Damn Blake always being so close and
          protective around me. Fuckers got to
          learn that I'm not like that, learn to
          back off and step down. Tell me not to
          come to a party, like fuck you. I could
          have brought him out, let him meet some
          people and make new friends. Dude
          wouldn't know a good time if it rubbed
          up against his ass. Dude needs new
          friends; I can't be around him all the
          time.

He continues driving slowly up the twisted path.

                    DEREK:(CONT'D)
          Fuck this party sure is out there, this
          party better be worth it.

Suddenly something runs out of the woods and stops in front of
his car. Jennie is standing in the headlights, looking out of
breath. She slams her hands down on the hood of the car.

                    JENNIE:
          You have got to help me!

Derek puts his car in park and gets out. He stands there with the
door open. Shouting can be heard, and Jennie quickly darts off
into the woods.

CONTINUED:

                    DEREK:
          Jennie wait! What's going on?

He looks up ahead and sees a rabbit running towards him. It's a
man with a rabbit mask, and he's holding a shotgun. Derek goes to
get back into his car. The man with the shotgun approaches a
pulls the door open.

                    BLAKE/MR.RABBIT:
          Turn the car off and get out. Throw the
          keys to me.

Head down, Derek does what he says. Blake bends down to pick up
the keys. Derek takes the opportunity to rush Blake before he can
get a shot off. The wrestle and Derek manages to get Blakes mask
off, but Blake breaks free and manages to get the gun trained back
on Derek. They stare at each other in shock.

                    BLAKE/MR.RABBIT: DEREK:
          Derek. Blake.

Act 2.2

ACT 2.2

INT.POLICE STATION - CONTINUOUS

Officer Monroe walks through the front doors of the police
station, through the halls past the desk and cubicles and into his
office. He sits and his desk and flips through some files before
closing them. OFFICER THEODORE walks up and knocks on the door.

                    OFFICER MONROE:
          What is it?

                    OFFICER THEODORE:
          Just want to let you know that we
          followed up on the missing teacher's
          case.

                    OFFICER MONROE:
          And what did you find out?

                    OFFICER THEODORE:
          All victim's family say that they
          reported having to say late the night
          before at the school. Some sort of
          teachers meeting.

                    OFFICER MONROE:
          And did you follow up on that.

                    OFFICER THEODORE:
          We did but there are no reports that the
          teachers even entered the school at that
          time. None of the other teachers got a
          report of a meeting. We're at a dead
          end.

                    OFFICER MONROE:
          Clearly, you're not working hard enough.
          You're not getting paid to sit around on
          your ass and ask all the wrong questions.
          Don't you think it's strange that it was
          a teacher meeting for our four people. I
          want you to go back to the house and
          drill the families, someone's got to
          know where the teachers went to.

Officer Theodore stands in the doorway, waiting for his boss to be
finished.

CONTINUED:

                    OFFICER MONROE:(CONT'D)
          Well, why are you just standing there,
          get moving.

Officer Theodore goes to leave but is stopped when Officer Monroe
speaks up again.

                    OFFICER MONROE:(CONT'D)
          Your sons the prom King and Silver Creek
          is he not?

                    OFFICER THEODORE:
          Yes, he is, why do you ask?

                    OFFICER MONROE:
          Just curious, did he mention a party
          being hosted tonight in his honor?

                    OFFICER THEODORE:
          Not that I'm aware of, why?

                    OFFICER MONROE:
          No reason, just following up on something
          I had seen earlier.

Officer Theodore leaves the room and back out into the hall,
Officer Monroe pulls the letter out of his pocket and carefully
examines it over.

                    OFFICER MONROE:(CONT'D)
          Oh, Brian please tell me you're not
          getting yourself in over your head.

INT.FARMHOUSE - CONTINUOUS.

Mike stands, Brian's gun held firmly in his good hand. He's
pointing in at Brian who is unarmed, Miranda and Stacy have their
guns on him. Brian holds out his hands like a man ready to
surrender.

                    BRIAN/MR.WOLF:
          Everyone just take it easy. No need to be
          firing off bullets at each other, nobody
          needs to die.

                    MIKE:
          Funny. You say nobody needs to die but
          look around you. Look at what you've done
          to us. You say we're the monsters but
          you're no better than we are. You should
          have killed us.

CONTINUED:

                    MIKE: (cont'd)
          when you had the chance. Looks like I'm
          in control now.

                    BRIAN/MR.WOLF:
          I said drop the gun, you go firing that
          thing and they will kill you. You don't
          need to die today; you can still go
          home.

                    MIKE:
          No, we negotiate on my terms now.

                    BRIAN/MR.WOLF:
          And what would that be?

                    MIKE:
          Take off your masks first, I want to see
          who exactly is behind all this.

                    BRIAN/MR.WOLF:
          Now you don't really think we are going
          to do that, are you. How about this you
          lower the gun, then I'll take off my
          mask.

                    MIKE:
          No deal, take off the mask or I'll start
          firing.

Mike begins to get dizzy; he closes his eyes, placing his hands on
his head trying to stop his sudden migraine. He is getting dizzy
from the loss of blood. Brian takes the advantage and rushes
towards him; Mike manages to regain his balance and quickly
steadies his aim. Brian stops short.

                    MIKE:(CONT'D)
          Thought you almost had me there didn't
          you. I suggest you hurry up and do as I
          say, I'm getting dizzy over here and I
          might start shooting.

                    BRIAN/MR.WOLF:
          Ok, just calm down. Look here you see,
          I'm going to reach up and take off my
          mask now.

                    MIRANDA/MS.SHEEP:
          Are you mad, you serious about showing
          him your face. Why don't we just shot him
          now and be done with it.

CONTINUED:

Mike is getting a little more uneasy.

                    BRIAN/MR.WOLF:
          No, nobody needs to die here today. Just
          everybody stay calm.

                    STACY/MS.CHICKEN:
          We weren't to reveal our faces, we were
          supposed to make it out without getting
          caught.

                    BRIAN/MR.WOLF:
          Change of plan, you can still make it
          out. He wants to see my face then so be
          it, if nobody gets killed it's what I'll
          do.

                    STACY/MS.CHICKEN:
          Fine if you do it then I'm doing it too,
          we'll all go done together.

                    MIRANDA/MS.SHEEP:
          Same with me.

                    BRIAN/MR.WOLF:
          Fine then, we do this together.

Brian reaches up and takes off his mask, Stacy does the same.
However, she has to lower her gun to do so, Stacy goes over and
takes Mirandas off for her making sure Miranda is still able to
keep her gun on Mike. Those who are able sit up to look at the
faces of those who hold them hostage.

                    MIKE:
          Brian, you're behind all this? You weak
          little fuck, this was all your doing.
          Should have figured you were behind all
          this, always thought one day you would
          snap. And Stacy should have known it was
          you. The masks all make since now.

                    BRIAN:
          I don't see how you didn't realize it was
          her from the beginning. She wanted to
          wear those masks for a reason, I figured
          you would have clued in right away.

                    STACY:
          I told him that you wouldn't know who I
          was or any of us were. To full of
          yourselves to remember

                    (MORE)

                                              (CONTINUED)

CONTINUED:

                    STACY: (cont'd)
          those you have hurt. I figured I wear
          the chicken mask, since I would have been
          the only one to know about the man off
          screen wearing it. But no, you couldn't
          even recognize my voice.

                    MIKE:
          And fat Miranda, why are you all doing
          this?

                    BRIAN:
          Cause of the countless things you've
          done to us. The beatings in the shower,
          breaking me down, making me feel like I
          was never good enough to do anything.
          Always breaking my will. So, I thought
          I'd break yours, doesn't feel good when
          you're on the other side does it. Not
          used to people standing up against you.

                    MIKE:
          Standing you against us, is that what you
          call this? We bullied you, so you
          tortured us.

                    STACY:
          You don't think you tortured us, you
          raped me. Defiled me, then sent it out to
          be broadcasted all over the school. You
          humiliated me, I started taking pills
          because of you. Try to drown out my own
          screams in my head.

                    MIRANDA:
          And the pretty girls, all I ever wanted
          was to be your friend. But you spit in my
          food, rubbed my face in shit. Call me
          fat. Because of you I don't feel like I
          belong anywhere, I look in the mirror
          and I'm not proud of what I see. I
          disgust myself, and you made me think
          that way. I try to change myself and for
          what, just so I can be one of those
          girls that everybody wants to be with. I
          decided that you needed to see what I see
          when I look in the mirror,

                         (MORE)

                                        (CONTINUED)

CONTINUED:

                    MIRANDA: (cont'd) what will
          you become when you no longer have
          your beauty.

                    MIKE:
          And the fourth guy, who is that?

                    BRIAN:
          Someone else you've hurt.

                    MIKE:
          So, you four mental cases planned this
          all by yourself? And the teachers, did
          you do something to them as well.

                    STACY:
          As much as they deserve to be in the same
          position that you are in, no their
          disappearance has nothing to do with us.

By this time Serena has gone from scratching her face to looking
up at what is going on. She notices finally that her captures don't
have their masks on. She hasn't been paying attention to the
conversation.

                    SERENA:
          They'd shown us their faces, were surely
          going to die now. They never let the
          hostages live once they have revealed
          themselves to them.
          Mike, you got a gun why aren't you
          shooting. Kill them for what they did to
          me.

                    BRIAN:
          For what we did to you, lady stop and
          think for a moment about all the things
          we have done tonight. Mike beats me up,
          breaks me down so I break his hand. I cut
          your face, to make him feel helpless.

                    STACY:
          Chris's eyes because he filmed my rape.
          John and Henry having sex, forced rape
          just the way they like it.

                    MIRANDA:
          Burning the skin off your face, making
          you ugly. Forcing you to eat

                         (MORE)

                                             (CONTINUED)

CONTINUED:

                    MIRANDA: (cont'd) makeup
          cause it's the inside that
          counts the most right, no matter how ugly
          you are on the outside you will always
          be prettier on the inside. Making Kelsey
          eat dog shit, it doesn't taste too good
          does it.

                    BRIAN:
          You see, everything we did tonight was
          because of something you did to us or
          made us feel. Your actions don't go
          without consequences.

                    MIKE:
          My actions, let me tell you a little
          story about actions and consequences.
          Your dad and my dad, both cops, well back
          when they were in high school about our
          age they both attended Silver Creek high.
          Now my dad was a big nerd, looking at me
          and how I turned out you probably
          wouldn't believe it but it's true. Back
          in the day my father had this one kid at
          school, used to pick on him continuously.
          His name was Bret Monroe.

Brian looks at him puzzled, he starts to shake his head.

                    BRIAN:
          My dad, you're saying my dad used to
          bully around your dad.

                    MIKE:
          Bully. Your dad used to corner my dad in
          the locker room, beat the shit out of
          him. Make him hand over his lunch money,
          stuffed him in lockers. Well then one
          day, Becky Swanson asked my dad to the
          prom, and he was head over heels for this
          woman. She was the top broad to be with
          in our school. People envied my dad, how
          did someone as nerdy as him land such a
          smoking hot babe.
          Well prom was a few weeks away, and up to
          that point Becky and my dad were going
          pretty steady. Hell he lost his virginty
          to her in the back seat of the limo on
          the way to the dance. At the dance My
          father

                    (MORE)

                                        (CONTINUED)

CONTINUED:

                    MIKE: (cont'd)
     gets out with his date and they couldn't
     be happier, they dance they sing, they
     kiss. It's like a princess story except
     my dad is the princess. My dad excuses
     himself to go to the bathroom, while at
     the stall your dad and his friends
     corner him. They toss him around a bit
     and lock him in the janitor's closet for
     the night. Your dad goes and tells Becky
     that her date took off, didn't want to
     be around her. She breaks down crying
     and of course your dad is there to
     comfort her. And just like the girl she
     is, she jumps on your dad like she won a
     prize. Now ladies and gentlemen do any
     of you want to venture a guess as to who
     Becky Swanson is?

                    BRIAN:
     She. She's my mom.

                    MIKE:
     Bingo. She's your mother. Now you see
     why I call her a whore. You understand
     me a little more. Now back to the story,
     years past and my dad joins the police
     academy and becomes an officer. He meets
     a girl at a cafe, they marry and have a
     son.
     Everything is going great, until your
     dad moves back into town. Low and behold
     he's an officer as well. My dad thinks
     great this is my chance I can get
     payback for all those years of torment.
     But something about your dad is
     different, he isn't the same man he used
     to be. So, years go by, and they get
     along great until one day. Your mother
     dies is a car accident, drunk driver.
     Your dad is distraught, but that doesn't
     stop him from tracking down the man
     behind the wheel who killed his wife. The
     drunk driver turned out to be behind a
     string of convenience store robberies in
     the area, biggest bust of your dads
     career. Since under the circumstances of
     what happened to his wife, and the bust
     he made.

                         (MORE)

                                             (CONTINUED)

CONTINUED:

                    MIKE: (cont'd)
          the higher ups decide to promote him.
          He's now head over my dad, and sure
          enough within weeks the power hunger
          sets in and it's just like high school
          again. Except my dad doesn't stand up to
          him, no he's got a 10-year-old at home
          he can take it out on. And since then,
          bad days at work mean a bad day at home.
          I grew up, became prom King, captain of
          the football team. But still no matter
          how strong I am my dad the coward would
          beat me.

                    BRIAN:
          So, you beat me because your dad beat
          you.

                    MIKE:
          No, I beat you because your dad is the
          reason why my dad beats me.

                    BRIAN:
          So why are you telling me this now, not
          once have you ever mentioned this about my
          dad.

                    MIKE:
          Because as much of a monster as you think
          I am I never wanted to take away the
          respect and love you had for your dad.
          Something I wish I had. A father who
          didn't hit me.
          Sure, I was pissed, I envy that your dad
          doesn't hit you. But because of him, my
          dad made me the way I am today. Maybe in
          another life we could have been friends,
          but this life is different. It's a
          vicious circle out there, when you think
          of it were only here in this room
          because of our parents.

                    STACY:
          So, you want to blame your dad for
          beating you that's fine, that doesn't
          explain why you raped me.

                    MIKE:
          Honestly, I don't have an answer for that.
          We all make stupid mistakes.

CONTINUED:

                    STACY:
          So, it's a stupid mistake, you know I
          came here in hope to make myself feel
          better. To get some closure, but I only
          feel worse. I don't think I can do this
          anymore.

Brian slowly walks up to Mike.

                    BRIAN:
          Just drop the weapon, you've got what
          you wanted. You've seen our faces, now
          just give me the gun.

He holds out his hands, but Mike reacts by firing the gun into the
ceiling. Brian jumps back.

                    MIKE:
          No, you get back and you stay back, I
          need Stacy to bring over the keys and
          unlock us. Next, I'll need you to put
          them on and wait for your friend to show
          up when he does, you tell him to drop his
          gun and lock himself up too. Once we are
          free, we ae going to take our keys and
          leave, wither or not you get out of here
          before the police come is up to you.

                    MIRANDA:
          In case you haven't realized I still have
          a gun; we're not doing anything you say.
          You drop the gun; we walk out of here,
          that's how this is going to play out.

Mike is on edge now, his loss of blood causing him to lose his
balance and he falls to one knee. Brian takes this as a sign to
wrestle the gun out of his hand, so he runs forth, Mikes quick
reacting he fires dead center into Brians chest. Brian stumbles
backwards and onto the floor, Stacy rushes to his aid.

                    STACY:
          Brian! Brian! Brian answer me, please
          Brian please.

The door to the barn swings open, Mike running on adrenaline shoots
at the door as it opens. Derek is the first person walking through
the door, he takes the bullet in the shoulder. He collapses to the
ground as Blake (who is still wearing his mask) drops his gun to
hold Derek.

Miranda fires her gun shooting Mike just above the right arm. He
falls backwards, gun slides across the floor and out of his hands.
Everyone is screaming, some are holding their ears others are
closing their eyes wishing for it to stop.

EXT- FARMHOUSE WOODS - SAME.

Blake has his gun still aimed at Derek; they both stand there with
their mouths open. To stunned to move.

                    DEREK:
          Blake, what going on? Why do you have a
          gun?

                    BLAKE:
          I told you not to come to the party, you
          weren't supposed to be here.

                    DEREK:
          And I decided to come, apparently, I
          should have stayed home. Now answer the
          question why are you running around with
          a gun.

                    BLAKE:
          I can't answer that.

                    DEREK:
          Why not, what are you doing up there?
          Why was Jennie running away scared?
          What's going on at the party?

                    BLAKE:
          It's complicated. What we're doing is
          complicated.

                    DEREK:
          What we're doing! How many more of you
          are up there?

                    BLAKE:
          Three. Me, Stacy, Miranda and Brian.

                    DEREK:
          Who else is up there with you besides
          Jennie.

CONTINUED:

                    BLAKE:
          about six others.

                    DEREK:
          She seemed scared. What are you doing to
          those people up there.

                    BLAKE:
          Teaching them a lesson. Showing them
          what it's like to be hurt, punishing
          them for their wrongdoings.

                    DEREK:
          Ok Blake this is starting to creep me
          out. I'm going to leave.

Blake cocks his shotgun; he shows betrayal on his face but he has
to do what he has to do. Blake grabs his mask and puts it back
on.

                    DEREK:(CONT'D)
          So, you're going to shot me is that it.

                    BLAKE:
          Not if I don't have to but I'm not
          letting you leave, you're coming back
          with me to the house.

Blake walks behind Derek and ushers him forward with a poke from
the gun into his back. Derek proceeds to move up the trail when a
loud scream can be heard coming from further down the trail. They
both turn in the direction.

                    DEREK:
          That sounded like Jennie.

                    BLAKE:
          That it did.

Blake and Derek both run in the same direction, through the thick
branches of trees. Jennie screams again, this time they're
getting closer. They stop when they come across Jennies frail
frame standing in the middle of the woods.
Derek steps on a tree branch and it cracks. Jennie turns her head,
frantic.

                    JENNIE:
          You stay away from me, don't come any
          closer.

CONTINUED:

                    DEREK:
          Now just calm down, we're here to help
          you. Were heard your screams coming from
          the trail.

                    JENNIE:
          You don't understand, you shouldn't have
          come. They're hurting people up there.

                    DEREK:
          Who is? What's going on up there?

                    JENNIE:
          They tortured us, they got us chained up.
          They made boys have sex with each other,
          they burned Stacy's face, broke Mikes
          hand.
          It's a massacre up there. They let me go,
          I ran for help will I got my leg caught
          in one of their traps.

Derek and Blake look down, Jennie has her leg caught in a bear
trap like the one they used but older. Derek turns to Blake.

                    DEREK:
          You did this to these people?

                    BLAKE:
          Not this one, this one isn't ours. Looks
          like it could be a trap left behind by
          the last owner of this place. Honestly,
          we didn't do this, she just happened to
          have a bad stroke of luck I guess.

                    DEREK:
          You got her into this mess you going to
          help her out of it.

                    BLAKE:
          No, you're going help her out of it then
          you're going to carry her back to the
          house.

                    DEREK:
          But she needs to get medical attention.

                    BLAKE:
          And I assure you we will call for an
          ambulance when we get there.

CONTINUED:

Blake motions with the gun for Derek to help Jennie, he does so
and manages to set her foot free. Her ankle is broken, skin is
torn, and blood is running down her shoes. Derek picks her up and
carries her out of the woods and back to the trail with Blake
close behind him.

                    JENNIE:
          Please don't take me back there.

                    DEREK:
          I'm sorry but I have to. I promise though
          that no more harm will befall you
          tonight.

They are halfway up the trail when they hear the first gunshot.

                    DEREK:
          That sounded like a gun.

                    BLAKE:
          This probably can't be good.

They run up the rest of the trail as fast as they can and stop by
the parked cars. Blake motions to Derek to stay. They hear some
commotion going on inside, sounds like Mike has gotten a gun from
one of the others.

                    BLAKE:(CONT'D)
          Stay here I'm going in.

                    DEREK:
          Fuck that, if people in there need help,
          I'm going in.

The second shot goes off, screaming can be heard.

                    STACY:
          Brian! Brian! Brian answer me, please
          Brian please.

Derek has laid Jennie on the ground and goes running up to the
door. Blake takes off after him.

                    BLAKE:
          Derek wait up you can't go in there just
          yet.

Derek flings the door open and is greeted with a bullet to the
shoulder. He collapses to the ground. The third shot goes off from
Mirandas gun hitting Mike. Derek takes off his mask to get a
better look at Derek's injury.

CONTINUED:

                    BLAKE:(CONT'D)
          Derek. Derek, come on man answer me.
          Damnit Derek it's just a flesh wound.

It is more than just a flesh wound. Blood squirts out of his
shoulder drenching the ground and Blakes hands. Blake slaps him
across the face trying to get Derek to wake up.

                    BLAKE:(CONT'D)
          Come on man you can do this. Wake up,
          just wake up for me.

He begins to perform Cpr on Derek, pounding on his chest for him to
revive.

                    BLAKE:(CONT'D)
          Why won't you wake up!

He continues to pound on his chest and blow air into his mouth. He
grows tired, the last bit of air he blows into Derek's mouth turns
into a kiss. He lingers before pulling back, tears filled in his
eyes.

                    BLAKE:(CONT'D)
          You weren't supposed to be here. He was
          the only exception; he wasn't supposed
          to be here.

He's cradling Derek's head in his arms.

INT.FARMHOUSE - CONTINUOUS.

Stacy is also trying to slap Brian awake from being shot. She
places her head on his chest, it's still moving. With a large
gasp for air Brain jerks upright. Sore he begins to rub his
chest.

                    STACY:
          Oh, thank god your alive, I thought I
          lost you.

                    BRIAN:
          For a moment I thought I was going to die
          too. Thank God I wore my dad's bullet
          proof vest.

                    STACY:
          You're wearing a vest?

                                              (CONTINUED)

CONTINUED:

                    BRIAN:
          For extra protection, I needed it. Looks
          like I did.

Blake come in like a mad man, still crying he lifts Brian up off
the floor.

                    BLAKE:
          You were wearing a vest and you didn't
          even care to give us one. What if we were
          shot? Did you ever think of that.

                    BRIAN:
          My dad only has one.

                    BLAKE:
          So, you figured you keep it a secret from
          us is that it. Wouldn't have cared if any
          of us got shot as long as you were
          protected.

Stacy tried to come between them and pull them apart, Blake just
shoves her aside.

                    STACY:
          Blake just calm down, it was his vest he
          can use if he wants to.

                    BLAKE:
          Stay out of this Bitch. My friend just
          died because he was shot, because of
          your fucking stupid little revenge party
          you got going on here. Why should he have
          to die, and this fuck gets to live.

Brian looks over at Derek's body in the doorway.

                    BRIAN:
          I'm sorry about your loss but this wasn't
          my fault.

                    BLAKE:
          You provided us with the guns.

                    BRIAN:
          The gun he was shot with was yours.

                    BLAKE:
          What did you say?

CONTINUED:
                         BRIAN:
               The six shooter you lent me. Mike got
               his hands on it. That's what he shoot
               Derek with. It wasn't my guns it was
               yours that killed him.

Blake lets go of Brian. He looks around the room and finds the
gun that Mike had dropped. He checks the chamber, only two bullets
left.

He stands there and stares at the others.

                         BLAKE:
               So, I killed him.

                         STACY:
               This isn't your fault don't go blaming
               yourself. This was all Mikes doing.

                         MIRANDA:
               What was Derek doing here anyway? I
               thought you told him not to come.

                         BLAKE:
               I did, guess he decided not to listen to
               me.

Blake walks over and stands over Mike who is bleeding from his
shoulder as well.

                         BLAKE: (CONT'D)
               Almost the same place as Derek got shot.
               How is it that scum like you still manage
               to hang on and grasp for life, yet good
               people get there's taken away from them.

                         MIKE:
               Go fuck yourself you fruit loop, should
               have guess you were the fourth person
               behind all this. Makes sense that you
               would want two men to fuck each other,
               must have turned you on did it.

Blake aims his gun and Mikes head.

                         MIKE: (CONT'D)
               We going to be a tough guy now. Go
               ahead, finish me. Pull that trigger.
               Just so you know I wasn't aiming for your
               friend I was aiming for you.

                                                         (CONTINUED)

CONTINUED:

                    STACY:
          Blake, what are you doing?

                    BLAKE:
          Taking out the trash.

                    STACY:
          Just put away the gun, nobody is supposed
          to die remember.

Blake laughs at this comment, he turns to her.

                    BLAKE:
          You're right, nobody was supposed to die
          tonight but somebody did. From the
          beginning we were way over our heads with
          this.

                    BRIAN:
          I know you're hurting but be rational
          about this. He's the one that killed
          Derek not us.

                    BLAKE:
          And he'll get away with it too. Cops
          will call it self-defense; he'll walk
          away with murder while we rot in a
          prison cell. Now this has gone far
          enough, we need to end this now.

                    MIRANDA:
          Who said anything about going to prison.

                    BLAKE:
          Don't be so naive, they've seen all our
          faces there's nothing to keep them
          quite.

                    SERENA:
          I knew they were going to kill us. Oh
          please, oh please, oh please don't kill
          us.

Blake backhands her with the gun, she slumps forward in and out of
consciousness.

                    BLAKE:
          Silence you filthy whore. I'm the only
          one in charge now, if you die it's
          because I pulled the trigger.

                                                              (CONTINUED)

CONTINUED:

                    STACY:
          Just take it easy, think about what
          you're doing.

                    BLAKE:
          I always think about what I do. Did you
          know that the other night I sat at home
          with this very gun, and I played Russian
          roulette with myself. Hoping that I could
          blow my own brains out, give my dad a
          real mess to clean up. But I chickened
          out, I couldn't take my own life.
          So, I went online and after seeing all
          the hateful things these monsters put
          online about me, I began to make a list.
          A hit list of every person I was going to
          kill the next day at school, and I loaded
          my gun and got on the bus with it the
          next day. At school Mike and his boys
          cornered me in the bathroom and I was
          about to pull out my gun when Derek came
          in. And just something about him, coming
          to my aid made me see the good in the
          world. He stopped me from causing a
          school shooting. And I knew that night I
          couldn't have done it anyway, I'm not a
          killer. Even here seeing what you guys
          did to these people, I never did
          anything as twisted as what you did. I
          don't even know why I'm here, all I did
          was suggest two men fuck and I filmed it
          but even as I stood up there, I wonder
          what was wrong with me why am I doing
          this to them. And I thought about Derek,
          my best friend. He was the only one that
          truly understood me, he stopped me from
          becoming a monster. So you're right
          Stacy, I do think before I do something.

He lowers the gun; Mike lets out a huge sigh of relief.

                    BLAKE: (CONT'D)
          But then again, what I think about is no
          longer here. I'm free to be that
          monster.

CONTINUED:

He lifts the gun back up and empties the remaining two bullets
into Mikes face, blood splatters up and all over Serena and John
as well as the floor.

                    STACY/BRIAN/MIRANDA:
          No!

                    STACY:
          What have you done?

                    BLAKE:
          embracing my inner demons.

                    JENNIE:
          Oh my god, he's just shot him. He's dead.

They turn towards Jennie who has managed to crawl towards Derek's
body and dug through his pockets for his phone. She is lying
there by the door with the phone up in her ear.
Blake walks over and rips the phone out of her hands. The operator
can be heard from the other end.

                    OPERATOR:
          Miss, can you still hear me, are you
          still there? Miss? Miss?

Blake hangs up the phone and smashes it on the floor.

                    BLAKE:
          Looks like we'll be having company folks.

INT.POLICE STATION - CONTINUOUS

Officer Monroe and Theodore and sitting in the briefing room when
one of the SECRETARYS comes in.

                    SECRETARY:
          Sargent, a word.

                    OFFICER MONROE:
          Yes, come on in, have a seat.

                    SECRETARY:
          We just got a call from a young girl
          named Jennie Miles. She was in distress
          when she called, the operator said she
          was being held hostage by a group of
          four individuals. Says they are being
          held in a farmhouse, being tortured.

                                        (CONTINUED)

CONTINUED:

                    OFFICER THEODORE:
          That's one of Mikes girlfriends'
          friends. She's on the cheerleading team.
          Did she give her address?

                    SECRETARY:
          No just that, the operator asked her who
          was holding her hostage and before she
          could answer there were two-gun shots
          and Jennie said someone killed someone
          and then the line went dead.

                    OFFICER MONROE:
          Did you run a trace of the phone?

                    SECRETARY:
          We're working on it now, the phone
          belongs to a Derek Grant.

                    OFFICER THEODORE:
          Derek Grant? That's another one of the
          popular kids from Mikes school.

                    OFFICER THEODORE:
          Cindy get us a trace on that cell as
          soon as possible, I want all the police
          out searching every farm house in the
          county. We need to get a move on, let's
          go.

The secretary leaves the room.

                    OFFICER THEODORE:
          Do you think this has anything to do with
          the missing teachers?

                    OFFICER MONROE:
          Teachers and now students. Something
          isn't right with this picture; I have a
          feeling things ae about to get a lot
          worse.

INT.FARMHOUSE - CONTINUOUS.

Blake grabs Jennie by the hair of the head and cuffs her next to
Henry. He drags Derek's body and gun and places them beside the
door. He shuts the door and locks it back up. Serena is slowly
coming too, she notices the blood on her face and begins to freak
out. She turns to Mikes dead body.

                                                      (CONTINUED)

CONTINUED:

                    SERENA:
          Mike, mike. Baby wake up.

                    BLAKE:
          He's dead, he isn't waking up.

                    SERENA:
          You're all monsters, every one of you.

                    BLAKE:
          Bitch I suggest you shut up before I come
          over there and begin to peel that burnt
          skin from your face.

Brian walks over and grabs Blake by the shoulder, Blake turns and
shoves him off.

                    BLAKE:(CONT'D)
          Don't try to sympathize with me, you and
          girlfriend is what got us into this mess
          in the first place.

                    BRIAN:
          This is going way too far. You've just
          killed a man; we weren't supposed to do
          that.

                    BLAKE:
          Oh but torturing them is ok is it, what
          you've done to these people there better
          off being dead. I've played by your
          rules Brian, now we play by mine. First,
          I think we start with little miss
          chatter box over here.

Blake pulls out a knife and wields it in front of Jennies face.
He pinches her cheeks.

                    BLAKE:(CONT'D)
          Stick out your tongue.

She shakes her head no, crying she tries to pull her face away.

                    BRIAN:
          What are you doing?

                    BLAKE:
          Teaching her that it's not ok to rat on
          people.

CONTINUED:

                    STACY:
          Blake just leave her alone, the police
          will be here any minute. If you stay
          we'll get caught.

                    BLAKE:
          Fine then leave but I'm staying, I'm not
          finished with them yet.

                    MIRANDA:
          Were in this together, you must come with
          us.

                    BLAKE:
          If were in this together then it looks
          like you're staying until I'm done.

He squeezes Jennies face harder, digging his nails into the side
of her face. He pokes her tongue out a little bit enough for Blake
to grab ahold of it with two fingers.

                    BLAKE: (CONT'D)
          You see this is what happens to people in
          prison when you start ratting to the
          cops.

She screams, but Blake slides the knife across her tongue slowly.
It's dull so he takes his time cutting. Henry who is sitting beside
her pukes. Blake tosses the severed tongue into her face; she too
begins to puke up blood as she makes her mumbled cry.

                    MIRANDA:
          Blake, what the hell is wrong with you?

                    BLAKE:
          Mad,   satanic,   psychotic,   really
          there's quite a few things wrong with
          me.

                    MIRANDA:
          You just cut out her tongue.

                    BLAKE:
          Yet none of you tried to stop me, so
          who's really to blame here.

                    BRIAN:
          Ok you've had your fun now let's go.

                    BLAKE:
          Fun, oh I've only just begone. I just
          found a part of myself and quite frankly
          I like the new me. Makes me wish I knew
          him sooner.

                    STACY:
          This right here, what you're doing is
          disgusting.

                    BLAKE:
          Says the girl who organized the whole
          thing. It's funny isn't it, how when we
          first came here it was you guys that
          wanted to do it, now it looks like you're
          becoming chickens and I'm the one leading
          the group. Maybe I should have been the
          one wearing the wolf mask, leader of the
          pack.

                    BRIAN:
          You're crazy.

                    BLAKE:
          You say crazy, I say creatively insane.

Blakes phone goes off in his pocket, he takes it out and ventures
away from the group. At the same time Stacy gets a message as well.

Blake has a video message from a number he doesn't recognize.

                    BLAKE:(CONT'D)
          Well, who could this be from.

He opens the video and stares at what appears to be the school
earlier that day. Brian is walking down the hall in the same
clothes he was wearing; he walks past a locker and slips an
invitation into it. The video doesn't last no longer for more
than twenty seconds. Just enough time for Blake to make out that
it was Derek's locker. He drops his phone and rushes over to
Brian, with one hit he punches Brian across the face with causes
Brain to stumble back against the wall.

                    BRIAN:
          What the fuck man?

CONTINUED:

                    BLAKE:
          Earlier when I asked you who put the
          letter in Derek's locker you said you
          didn't know.

                    BRIAN:
          And I don't know.

                    BLAKE:
          Then tell me why I just got a video from
          someone showing you walking over to
          Derek's locker and slipping in an
          invitation.

They all looked confused and stunned at Blakes accusation.

                    BRIAN:
          I don't know what you're talking about.

Blakes runs over and picks up his phone, he shoves the phone into
Brians face and plays the video.

                    BLAKE:
          That's you on the camera, that was this
          morning. You invited Derek to the party;
          you got Derek killed.

                    BRIAN:
          I didn't mean to.

                    BLAKE:
          Tell me, tell me why you didn't mean to.

                    STACY:
          Because I told him too.

Blake turns to her now.

                    BLAKE:
          So, you put him up to this. Why? Why do
          you have to pick Derek?

                    STACY:
          Because I was ordered too.

                    BLAKE:
          By whom?

                    STACY:
          I can't tell you.

CONTINUED:

                    BLAKE:
          Tell me God damnit or I'll bludgeon your
          fucking face in.

                    STACY:
          I was ordered by the person who let us
          use this place. I was under strict
          authority to invite every popular kid
          including Derek. That was the catch to
          us having this place.

                    BLAKE:
          The same person you told us earlier that
          you said didn't know what was going on.
          That same person.

Blake turns back to Brian.

                    BLAKE:(CONT'D)
          You ever get the feeling like we're being
          set up.

                    BRIAN:
          We're not being set up.

                    BLAKE:
          So, I assume you knew all about this then,
          or is this all news to you as well.

                    BRIAN:
          I'm just hearing about this for the first
          time.

Blake holds out his hand.

                    BLAKE:
          Give me your phone.

                    STACY:
          What no I'm not giving it to you.

                    BLAKE:
          Give it to me please.

                    BRIAN:
          Just hand him over the phone.

Stacy places the phone in his hand. He flips through the messages
until he comes across the same number that appeared on his phone.

                                                  (CONTINUED)

CONTINUED:

                    BLAKE:
          You see this. She's been keeping in
          contact with the same person that just
          sent me that video of you.
          Still don't think we're being set up,
          Brian this person is trying to turn us
          against each other. And right now, it's
          working. Bring the students here, bring
          the one person that wasn't supposed to
          show up.
          Torture, for Christ sakes they threw in
          a wild card that would tear us apart.
          They wanted us to end up killing each
          other, get rid of the students Christ
          even the teachers are here. Were in over
          our heads, this from the beginning was
          all one person using us. Teachers die,
          bullies die, fuck if we happened to
          survive who's to say they don't sell us
          down river. We were getting played since
          the moment this all began. And the only
          person in this room that knew that it
          was going on was Stacy.

                    STACY:
          We're not being played; we can trust this
          person.

                    BLAKE:
          Oh, can we, then why did they send me
          that video of Brian putting the letter
          into Derek's locker. Sounds like he
          wants us to turn against each other.

He scrolls through the messages on her phone.

                    BLAKE: (CONT'D)
          And these messages: 'He's on his way'
          what's that supposed to mean. If I had
          looked through Derek's phone right now
          would I find this number in his phone
          telling him to go to the party. Sounds
          like a set up to me.

                    MIRANDA:
          You must agree it does sound pretty
          suspicious.

CONTINUED:

                    BLAKE:
          Thank you. So again, I ask who is the
          person you were talking to.

                    STACY:
          I'm not willing to give that
          information out. I can't break their
          trust.

                    BLAKE:
          Fine. If you won't tell me, I guess I'll
          just have to get it out of you by other
          means.

He pockets her cell phone and walks over to pick his shotgun up
from where he left it next to Derek's body. He comes back and aims
it at Brian.

                    BRIAN:
          Jesus, put down the gun.

                    BLAKE:
          I want answers and I'm willing to get
          them either way.

                    STACY:
          Please just put down the gun. You're one
          of us, you wouldn't shot your own kind.

Miranda has aimed her gun at Blake.

                    MIRANDA:
          Please Blake don't make me shoot you.

                    BRIAN:
          Don't shoot, besides man I'm wearing the
          vest. It's going to hurt like hell.

                    BLAKE:
          At close range with a shotgun, I think
          it'll do more than just hurt. But what do
          I know, are you as eager as I am to find
          out.

                    STACY:
          You don't want to do this.

                    BLAKE:
          Like you said, I'm one of you. And I'm
          not too keen on friendly fire.

CONTINUED:

He turns the gun and points to at Stacy.

                    BLAKE:(CONT'D)
          But I also don't like traitors either.

Brian jumps to pull the gun out of his hand but it's too late.
Blake pulled the trigger and shot Stacy square in the chest sending
her back up against the wall and finally she falls. Blake drops the
gun, overhead the sound of choppers can be heard outside. Faint
search lights can be seen coming in through the cracks on the
windows.

                    BLAKE:(CONT'D)
          Looks like the cavalry has arrived.

INT.POLICE STATION - SAME.

Police officers are running around the room frantic, looking for
any possible leads on the whereabouts of the students that are
being held hostage. Officer Monroe is sitting at his desk when
Officer Theodore comes into his office.

                    OFFICER THEODORE:
          I just called my son's cell, he isn't
          answering. We called Jennies parents and
          they said she went out with Serena
          Matthews and Kelsey Moore. When I called
          Serenas parents they said my son had
          come by in his car and picked her up.

                    OFFICER MONROE:
          So, you're thinking that they could be
          there with Jennie as well.

                    OFFICER THEODORE:
          Could be. I was just following up on
          what you said earlier about my son going
          to a party. Turns out he was invited to a
          party gone wrong. How did you know he was
          going out tonight anyway?

                    OFFICER MONROE:
          Lucky guess. Kids like yours, always out
          partying on a Friday night.

                    OFFICER THEODORE:
          Some guess then.

                                             (CONTINUED)

CONTINUED:
                    OFFICER MONROE:
          Listen I don't want you to lead this
          case. It's too personal, you could make
          the wrong calls get somebody killed.

                    OFFICER THEODORE:
          Like fuck I going to stand around while
          some freaks hurt my boy. I'm going to
          take them down.

                    OFFICER MONROE:
          I said you're not working on this case
          and that's final, get back to finding
          those missing teachers.

At the point the secretary has entered the room, she is holding a
piece of paper in her hands.

                    SECRETARY:
          We just traced Derek's last call. It
          binged off several towers in the area,
          but they managed to isolate it to one
          sector. Turns out in the area there is
          only one abandoned farmhouse. It quite
          out there, going to have to send choppers
          in to canvas the area.

                    OFFICER MONROE:
          Where's the location at?

                    SECRETARY:
          1228 Remington drive, the place is
          completely isolated, great place to hold
          people hostage.

                    OFFICER MONROE:
          Can I see it.

The secretary hands him over the piece of paper, he pulls out
the invitation he has and compares the address. Exact match.

                    OFFICER THEODORE:
          What's that you got there?

                    OFFICER MONROE:
          Nothing. I have to go home, tell the boys
          to suit up and meet me at the farmhouse.
          They are not to make a move until I get
          there, is that understood.

CONTINUED:

                    OFFICER THEODORE:
          Understood.

                    OFFICER MONROE:
          And you are to go no where's near the
          farm house. You are off this case.

                    OFFICER THEODORE:
          understood.

Officer Monroe drops the letters on his desk and takes off out of
the room. Officer Theodore picks up the invitation and examines
it.

                    OFFICER THEODORE:
          Fucking bastard knew. I'll have his badge
          for this.

He walks out into the hall and addresses the other officers.

                    OFFICER THEODORE:(CONT'D)
          Listen up, gather your gear and
          equipment and get some choppers in the
          skies. Officer Monroe left and placed me
          in charge. We're going into a hostile
          situation. So i'll needs snipers at the
          ready. We don't know what these people
          are packed with, so we'll have to be
          prepared. We're going in and were
          bringing these kids home alive, there
          captures. It's a shoot to kill order.

INT.BRIANS HOUSE - CONTINUOUS.

Officer Monroe races home, his sirens on as he bypasses every
light and every car on the street. He leaves his car running in
the yard and rushes in through the front door and down the
basement stairs. He fiddles with the safes combination until he
manages to get it open. He stands there looking at a safe with
missing guns and ammunition and missing vest. He drops to his
knees.

                    OFFICER MONROE:
          Oh god Brian what have you done.

Act 3

ACT THREE

INT.POLICE STATION - CONTINUOUS.

Officer Monroe has rushed straight back to his office, charging in
through the front door he is greeted only by the Secretary. The
station is empty of officers, he walks to the front counter, panic
and stress in his voice.

                    OFFICER MONROE:
          Where is everybody?

                    SECRETARY:
          They left just a few moments ago, all
          units heading out to the scene. I thought
          you left with them,

                    OFFICER MONROE:
          What? Why did they leave?

                    SECRETARY:
          Officer Theodore ordered all units,
          choppers and swat to the scene.

Officer Monroe slams his hands on her desk, she jumps straight up
out of her chair.

                    OFFICER MONROE:
          And why would he do that. I ordered him
          off the case.

                    SECRETARY:
          He   came   out   shouting   commands,   I
          thought you put him in charge of the
          team.

Officer Monroe heads out back towards his office, he walks in and
finds he invitation no longer on his desk. More panic sets in.

                    OFFICER MONROE:
          Fuck, fuck, fuck.

He heads towards the front door, the secretary following closely
behind him.

                    SECRETARY:
          Is everything alright?

                    OFFICER MONROE:
          No, everything is most certainly not
          alright.

Officer Monroe heads out the door and jumps into his squad car
and takes off. Tires screech as he pulls out of the driveway and
onto the road.

EXT.FARMHOUSE - CONTINUOUS.

Squad cars, armored vans with sirens on pull up the long trail. A
Helicopter is flying over the farmhouse, aiming its search lights
directly down upon it. Armed swat teams are getting out of the
vans, police officers out of their cars. The cars and vans are
angled amongst the hostages' cars that are already parked there.
The officers are stationed behind them to offer themselves
protection in case of flying bullets.

Officer Theodore starts giving orders to a SWAT LEADER to get his
men into position.

                    OFFICER THEODORE:
          I want swat team with snipers up along
          those tree lines on both sides of the
          door. They come out I want them to be
          close enough to take the shot without
          endangering all hostages they bring out
          with them.

                    SWAT LEADER:
          Copy that. Alright men, let's get into
          position.

Officer Theodore glances at the cars, he spots Mikes car.

                    OFFICER THEODORE:
          That's my sons car. Fuck sakes so he is
          in there. Alright people listen up, we
          have a hostage situation, we know of at
          least four unsubs in there. We don't
          know who they are so we can't identify
          who were dealing with. What I do know is
          my son is one of the hostages, we take
          this with extreme precision. We know one
          of the hostages is dead, let's make sure
          no more follow. Now I need first
          responder medical teams here asap, we
          have possible wounded that need immediate
          medical attention.

CONTINUED:

                    COPS:
          Sir yes sir.

The cops take their positions, Officer Theodore grabs his bullhorn
from his squad car. The Swat leader approaches him again.

                    SWAT LEADER:
          My men are all into position.

                    OFFICER THEODORE:
          Good.

He goes to raise the bullhorn to his lips.

                    SWAT LEADER:
          Sir, I don't mean to intrude but are you
          sure you can take the lead on this?

Officer Theodore lowers his bullhorn; he shot the swat leader an
ignorant look.

                    OFFICER THEODORE:
          What's that supposed to mean? Do you
          think I'm not a capable leader?

                    SWAT LEADER:
          I don't mean to offend, it's just... your
          son is one of the hostages. Are you sure
          you're not to wrapped up in this, do you
          think you can make the right calls.

                    OFFICER THEODORE:
          I'll let you know that the only reason
          I'm taking charge on this case is because
          my son is in there. Sargent Monroe placed
          me in charge, if he thinks I'm capable
          then I'm capable. This will not affect
          my judgement call; do I make myself
          clear.

                    SWAT LEADER:
          Yes sir, I'm just making sure I don't
          take orders due to clouded judgement.

                    OFFICER THEODORE:
          My orders are nothing to be concerned
          about. You just keep your men ready for
          when I give the order.

                                                        (CONTINUED)

CONTINUED:

Officer Theodore raises the bullhorn back up to his face.

                    OFFICER THEODORE:(CONT'D)
          Attention, we have the place
          surrounded. Come out with your hands up.

INT.FARMHOUSE - CONTINUOUS.

Brian is tending to Stacy's wounds, pressing down hard to try and
stop the flow of blood. Stacy is lying on the floor not moving,
barely breathing. Brian places his face close to her mouth to
check for the flow of air.

                    BRIAN:
          Good she's still breathing. Come on
          Stacy, I need you to wake up I need you
          to stay with me.

                    BLAKE:
          Don't bother, Bitch is as good as dead.

                    BRIAN:
          What the fucks wrong with you? You shot
          her, this wasn't how it was supposed to
          end like this.

Miranda still has her gun pointed at Blake. She is scared, she
doesn't want to hurt or kill anyone.

                    BRIAN:(CONT'D)
          Why are you just standing there? Shot
          him!

Blake turns to Miranda and slowly approaches her.

                    BLAKE:
          You going to pull the trigger? Think
          you're big enough to take someone else's
          life. Shot me and those cops will burst
          through that door, they will gun you down
          before you even have a chance to let the
          gun hit the floor.

                    MIRANDA:
          Please just stay back, don't come near
          me.

CONTINUED:

                    BLAKE:
          Are you scared of me? Thought we were
          friends, all of us.

                    MIRANDA:
          You're a monster.

                    BLAKE:
          So, I'm a monster now. Just like them is
          that it, you must really want to put me
          down. Go on shoot me.

He places the barrel of the gun to his chest.

                    BLAKE:(CONT'D)
          Go on I said shoot me. Pull the fucking
          trigger!

                    BRIAN:
          Shoot him!

                    SERENA:
          Kill the fucker!

                    BLAKE:
          DO AS THEY SAY AND FUCKING SHOOT ME!

Miranda flinches and drops the gun to the floor; Blake kicks it to
the side.

                    BLAKE:(CONT'D)
          That's what I thought.

The officer in charge outside is shouting through his bullhorn
again.

                    OFFICER THEODORE:
          I repeat, come out with your hands.

Serena begins yelling.

                    SERENA:
          Help, get us out of here.

Blake places his hands across her mouth.

                    BLAKE:
          Shut the fuck up, before I cut your
          tongue out too.

CONTINUED:

She nods and as soon as he lets go of her face she screams again.
Blake drop kicks her in the face, she is now fully passed out of
the floor.

                    BLAKE:(CONT'D)
          Anyone else wants to say something, speak
          up.

Nobody says anything, they just huddled and scared.

                    BRIAN:
          We need to think of a way to get out of
          here. We need to get Stacy to the
          hospital.

                    BLAKE:
          The police got this place surrounded, we
          step one foot out there and were all
          dead. Nobody is going anywhere.

                    KELSEY:
          You know you're not going to make it out
          alive right. That's Mikes father out
          there, he's going to put you all down.

                    BLAKE:
          when I've asked for your opinion, I'll
          fucking ask for it.

                    MIRANDA:
          I can't deal with this anymore, I don't
          want to go to jail.

She looks to the hostages, sympathetic.

                    MIRANDA:(CONT'D)
          I'm sorry for the pain I have caused.

                    KELSEY:
          You should feel sorry you fat pig, look
          what you did to us. We don't accept your
          sympathy, go to hell all of you.

Blake grabs out his knife and jumps Kelsey, he is sitting over her
straddling her. She tries to push him off. He grabs one of her
hands and pushes her arm upright stretching it out over her head.

CONTINUED:
                         BLAKE:
               I thought I said no speaking. You see
               people like you don't know when to shut
               their mouths. They let their actions and
               words flow, never thinking of their
               consequences.
               When we brought you here you had one
               thing to ask yourself, why am I here.
               It's because you don't know when to shut
               the fuck up. You're hurtful and
               inconsiderate even when your life is in
               danger.

He slowly presses the blade through her open palm. Blood pools
past the cuts as he pushes the blade deeper.

                         BLAKE: (CONT'D)
               Maybe next time you speak this will
               remind you before you open your filthy
               trap.

Kelsey is crying, trying to scream but Blake has managed to get
one of his knees pressed into her face. He pulls the knife back,
leaving a little hole in her hand that leads all the way through.
He wipes the blood off his knife on her face and then places it
back into his pocket.

He stands back up.

                         BLAKE: (CONT'D)
               You want to get out of here alive
               Miranda. I think I have an idea.

EXT.FARMHOUSE - CONTINUOUS.

Officer Monroe is pulling up the trail, he gets out of his vehicle
and runs up from the foot of the hill to Officer Theodore who is
speaking to another officer. Monroe pushes Theodore up against a
car, wrapping his hands around his throat.

                         OFFICER MONROE:
               What the hell do you think you're doing?
               I told you to wait back at the precinct.

                         OFFICER THEODORE:
               You're not in charge anymore. I'm taking
               control of this case. You're being
               stripped of your rank.

Two officers are pulling Monroe off him. Theodore straightens
himself and rubs the marks on his throat.

                                                    (CONTINUED)

CONTINUED:

                    OFFICER MONROE:
          What do you mean I'm no longer in
          charge? As your commanding officer I
          demand to know what is going on.

                    OFFICER THEODORE:
          You lost all rights and leadership when
          you withheld evidence.

                    OFFICER MONROE:
          What evidence?

                    OFFICER THEODORE:
          The letter on your desk, the invitation.
          Is that why you went home, your son is a
          part of this too isn't he? Figures, he's
          probably in on this. Is that why you
          tried to hide the invitation, is your
          son a killer?

                    OFFICER MONROE:
          My son is a victim in this as much as
          your son is. I know my boy, if he's in
          there he's in the same position as those
          hostages.

                    OFFICER THEODORE:
          We'll see. Officers escort this man off
          the premises.

The two OFFICERS escort Monroe to the foot of the hill. Monroe
screams as they drag him away.

                    OFFICER MONROE:
          Don't do something you're going to
          regret.

At the hill the officers let him go, they stand guard and order
him into his vehicle to leave. Monroe jumps behind the wheel. He
pulls out his cellphone and quickly dials his son's number. He
places the phone to his ear.

                    OFFICER MONROE:(CONT'D)
          Come on Brian, pick up. Answer the god
          damn phone.

INT.FARMHOUSE - CONTINUOUS.

Blake is opening the door of the barn and peeking out a small
crack to see the situation outside.

                    BLAKE:
          They have the place surrounded. Swat
          team is here, must expect snipers in
          amongst the tree lines.

                    MIRANDA:
          I don't think I can do this.

Blake turns to her, grabbing her shoulders he gives her a shake.

                    BLAKE:
          You said it yourself; you didn't want to
          go to jail. This is the only plan I have;
          trust me it'll work.

                    MIRANDA:
          They'll know it's me, they know were the
          ones doing this.

                    BLAKE:
          They don't know anything, if they did,
          they would have started to call us by
          name the moment they got here. If they
          knew who we were they would try to make a
          more personal connection with us. They
          don't know who we are yet, trust me this
          will work.

Brian has been looking at his phone, there's an incoming call. He
presses the end call button.

                    BRIAN:
          Maybe I should be the one to do this. She
          doesn't seem like she can handle it.

                    BLAKE:
          No you're staying here with me. Miranda
          baby, you can do this. You just got to
          pick Stacy up and carry her outside,
          armed officers will rush you but don't be
          alarmed. They will escort you past the
          cars and both you and Stacy can get a
          ride to the hospital. They'll think
                    (MORE)

CONTINUED:
                    BLAKE: (cont'd)
          we're letting some of the hostages go,
          all you have to do is act natural don't
          say anything and you'll make it out
          fine.

                    MIRANDA:
          What about you two, how are you guys
          getting out of here?

                    BRIAN:
          Don't worry about us, you just get
          yourself to safety. Make sure you get
          Stacy help.

                    MIRANDA:
          Brian...I don't think Stacy is going to
          make it.

                    BRIAN:
          Just get her out of here, she's strong
          she's been through worse. She's a
          survivor.

Miranda picks up Stacy, she struggles at first, but she manages to
lift her. Blake and Brian put their masks back on and open the
door, standing to the sides so snipers can't get a clear shot.

Miranda walks forth carrying Stacy as the exit the barn into the
light on the helicopters search lights.

EXT.FARMHOUSE - CONTINUOUS.

Miranda walks out mid-way between the farm and the cars. The Swat
team grab her and rushes her forward. Ambulance drivers have
arrived, they place Stacy on a gurney. They begin to intubate,
forcing air into her lungs.

                    AMBULANCE DRIVER #1:
          Her vitals are dropping, we need to
          sustain her and get her to the hospital
          now.

They rush her onto the back of the ambulance. Miranda goes to go
in with her. Officer Theodore grabs her by the arm.

                    OFFICER THEODORE:
          I need a moment of your time. Just need
          to ask a few questions, if that's ok. I
          know you've been through a lot tonight.

CONTINUED:
                    MIRANDA:
          I really must get going, I need to go
          with my friend to the hospital.

                    OFFICER THEODORE:
          This won't take long. Did you see who's
          doing this?

                    MIRANDA:
          No, they wore masks. We never seen their
          faces.

The ambulance driver pulls Miranda away from the cop.

                    AMBULANCE DRIVER #2:
          If she's coming with us she needs to
          leave now.

                    MIRANDA:
          I'm sorry officer, I must go.

                    OFFICER THEODORE:
          That's ok, I'll be sure to send an
          officer along to the hospital to ask any
          routine questions we have.

Miranda hopes in the back and they shut the door, the ambulance
takes off sirens blaring as they head down the trail.

Officer Theodore turns around; the door to the house is closed
again. He addresses the swat team leader.

                    OFFICER THEODORE:
          Did your men get a visual on the targets.

                    SWAT LEADER:
          That's a negative.

                    OFFICER THEODORE:
          God damnit. I need to know who were
          dealing with here people.

                    SWAT LEADER:
          We're still working on it.

Officer Theodore looks back in the direction that the ambulance
left.

                    OFFICER THEODORE:
          I want an officer posted outside their
          door. I want to know why they were chosen
          to be set free.

INT.FARMHOUSE - CONTINUOUS.

                    BRIAN:
So, what's the plan now? How are we
getting ourselves out of this one.

                    BLAKE:
I'm thinking. This isn't as easy as it
looks.

                    BRIAN:
Well just think of something and fast.

                    BLAKE:
Think of something? We wouldn't be in this
situation if it wasn't for you sticking
that letter in Derek's locker.

                    BRIAN:
It wasn't my idea, it was Stacy's.

                    BLAKE:
And that's why she's dying on her way to
the hospital.

                    BRIAN:
You didn't have to shot her; she was only
doing what she was told.

                    BLAKE:
Ya and by who, we don't even know who's
really running things around here. And
you know what I may not have had to shot
her, you could have easily had taken that
bullet yourself.

                    BRIAN:
I wish you had shot me; I'll never
forgive you for what you did.

                    BLAKE:
You want to be mad at me Brian, fine.
Hate me, pick up that gun and shot me. I
have no reason to live, I'm ready to
die. But can you really live with
yourself, killing someone. You're not
like me, you're afraid of the depths of
hell it'll drag you through. So go ahead
and hate me, I could always use a friend
in hell.

(CONTINUED)

CONTINUED:

                    BRIAN:
          Look, I'm sorry for what I did.

                    BLAKE:
          Hold your apologies till we get out of
          here.

Blake walks to the back of the room and opens the door to the room
holding the teachers. He gives one look at them and goes back to
Brian.

                    BLAKE:(CONT'D)
          I finally have an idea.

                    BRIAN:
          What is it?

                    BLAKE:
          The police haven't seen our faces yet,
          they have no idea who we are.

                    BRIAN:
          And?

                    BLAKE:
          To them there are still four people in
          here holding them hostage.

                    BRIAN:
          So?

                    BLAKE:
          We'll I think I just found a use for the
          teachers.

                    BRIAN:
          What do we need to do?

                    BLAKE:
          We start with these ones first. Duct tape
          their mouths shut, tie their hands behind
          their backs.

EXT.FARMHOUSE - CONTINUOUS.

The farmhouse door opens, the cops become alert and attentive. They
draw their weapons.

                    OFFICER THEODORE:
          Ok everybody hold your fire there coming
          out.

                                                      (CONTINUED)

CONTINUED:

Four masked figures come walking out, all wearing sheep, wolf,
chicken and rabbit masks. They are carrying the two handguns and
shot guns. Two figures, the rabbit and the wolf, have guns
pressed to the heads of two other figures who are standing in
front of them. Both have black bags over their heads.

                    SWAT LEADER:
          Looks like they're using hostages as
          shields.

                    OFFICER THEODORE:
          Drop your weapons and stand down, we
          will shoot you.

Talking to the swat leader.

                    OFFICER THEODORE:(CONT'D)
          Your men got a clear line of sight?

The Swat leader speaks into his radio.

                    SWAT LEADER:
          Do you have visual confirmation on the
          targets? Over.

The snipers in the trees line up their sights, the dots fitting
directly over the target's heads.

                    SWAT SNIPER:
          Roger that team leader. Targets are in
          sight, awaiting orders. Over.

                    SWAT LEADER:
          We're awaiting your orders.

                    OFFICER THEODORE:
          Put down your guns and let the hostages
          go.

The targets do not speak, they slowly approach and move forward.

                    OFFICER THEODORE:(CONT'D)
          If you have the shot, take it.

                    SWAT LEADER:
          Take the shot.

                    SWAT SNIPER:
          Roger that. Taking shot.

CONTINUED:

The targets move forward, then for a moment time seems to stop.
Muzzles flash in the night, the four individuals' heads snap back.
Blood and brains explode out from the sides of the heads. They
fall to the ground, guns drop. Masks covered in blood.

The two remaining individuals stand there shaking. Officers come to
their aid and rush them to safety. Officer Theodore rushes past
them and into the barn. Other cops kicking the dropped guns to the
side and checking for vitals on the four individuals.

Past the police cars, the cops let the two individuals take a seat
in the back of an ambulance. They take their hoods off, both Brian
and Blake sit there. Brian in shock, Blake has a small smile
creeping across his face.

Ambulance workers are attending to them, checking them over for any
signs if they were hurt.

INT.FARMHOUSE - CONTINUOUS.

Officer Theodore walks into the barn. He finds eight individuals
in the center of the room. Most are tied up with duct tape. One
girl lies knocked out. He surveys the carnage, broken legs, faces
burnt, eyes dripping blood. He covers his mouth, so he doesn't
puke. There's another individual lying on the floor closet to the
door, not chained to the others. He turns him over, it's Derek.
Officer Theodore looks back at the two others chained that are
passed out. He continues over to them.

His stomach reacts to the sight of his son, he pukes but wipes
the drool off on his sleeve. He creases his sons head, parting
his hair. Tears drip from his eyes out his son's face.

                    OFFICER THEODORE:
          My boy, what did they do to you.

He is crying, weeping hard.

                    OFFICER THEODORE:(CONT'D)
          My boy, my beautiful boy. Please come
          back to me, come back.

The officers leave him to cry, the others tend to those still
tied up. One of the officers rips the tape off of Henrys mouth.

                                                      (CONTINUED)

CONTINUED:

                    HENRY:
          You must get the bastards responsible for
          this.

                    OFFICER #1:
          We got those responsible, its ok. You're
          all safe now.

                    HENRY:
          No, you don't understand. Those weren't
          the people who hurt us. You killed the
          wrong people.

Officer Theodore gazes up from his mourning.

                    OFFICER THEODORE:
          What do you mean those weren't the ones.

Another officer from outside comes in.

                    OFFICER #2:
          Ah sir, you might want to come out here
          and have a look at this.

EXT.FARMHOUSE - CONTINUOUS.

Officer Theodore walks out to the four bodies. There lying
unmasked on the ground are the four missing teachers. Their mouths
and eyes were taped shut.

                    OFFICER THEODORE:
          So, the missing teachers were the ones
          behind all this?

                    OFFICER #2:
          It would appear we solved another case.
          It's strange. They came out wearing
          masks, but their eyes and mouths were
          shut so they couldn't see or speak.
          Their guns weren't even loaded, all
          empty.

                    OFFICER THEODORE:
          Why, why would they all have empty guns.
          Did they want to die?

                    OFFICER #2:
          That's the second strange thing. They
          have ear plugs in all their ears, none of
          them would have heard you tell them to
          back down.

                                              (CONTINUED)

CONTINUED:

Officer Theodore rushes back into the house. By now all the victims
have their hands untied and mouths untapped.
Ambulance workers are attending to the wounded.

He addresses Jennie.

                    OFFICER THEODORE:
          Sweetheart, you're the one who called
          us. Can you tell me for certain that
          those four individuals out there were the
          ones that attacked you.

Jennie mumbles. Officer #1

speaks up.

                    OFFICER #1:
          She can't talk sir. It appears that they
          cut her tongue out.

                    OFFICER THEODORE:
          Those sick fucks. Can any of you tell me
          for certain that those people out there
          lying on the ground were the ones that
          did this to you. That they were the ones
          that killed my boy.

                    JOHN:
          No, sir it wasn't them.

                    OFFICER THEODORE:
          Then who was it?

                    HENRY:
          It was Brian Monroe, Blake Gilmore, Stacy
          Lawrence and Miranda Osteen. Those were
          the people that did this.

                    OFFICER THEODORE:
          And where are they?

                    KELSEY:
          Those were the ones you let go, you
          killed the wrong people.

Officer Theodore turns to officer #1.

                    OFFICER THEODORE:
          Take me to where the two hostages that
          came out are at.

EXT.FARMHOUSE - CONTINUOUS.

Officer #1 leads officer Theodore to the ambulance. Officer
Theodore looks up at the ambulance worker in the back. He begins
to shout.

                    OFFICER THEODORE:
          Where are they?

                    AMBULANCE DRIVER #3:
          Who?

                    OFFICER THEODORE:
          The two hostages that were brought out,
          where are they?

                    AMBULANCE DRIVER #3:
          I don't know, I turned around and they
          were gone.

Officer Theodore turns to his officer.

                    OFFICER THEODORE:
          Find them, get out of my sight and find
          them. Send squads over the hospital you
          can find two of them there. The other
          two search for there vehicles in the
          area, they could be driving or walking.
          They couldn't have gotten far.

Officer Theodore hurries to the bottom of the trail while his men
jump into their cars and take off.

EXT.BOTTOM OF THE TRAIL - CONTINUOUS.

Officer Monroe is sitting by his car while squads' cars come
driving out of the trail and onto the road. Officer Theodore comes
up to him, hands clenched into a fist.

                    OFFICER MONROE:
          I heard the shots, what happened.

Officer Theodore draws his fist back and cracks Officer Monroe
across the face. His nose breaks.

                    OFFICER THEODORE:
          What happened? Your son is what happened.
          Where is he?

CONTINUED:

                    OFFICER MONROE:
          I don't know.

                    OFFICER THEODORE:
          You lie.

He brings his knee up into Monroe's stomach, the two officers
guarding the entrance try to come between them but Monroe tells
them to stop.

                    OFFICER MONROE:
          Don't this is between me and him.

They continue to fight; Monroe brings his foot down behind
Theodores leg causing it to give. On his knees Monroe grabs the
back of his head and bashes it into the side of his cruiser.
Theodores nose breaks, both now have blood pouring down their
chins. They continue to throw punches until Monroe manages to get
him into an arm and head lock. Theodore is unable to move.

                    OFFICER MONROE: (CONT'D)
          Now what happened?

                    OFFICER THEODORE:
          Your son, he and his puny band of
          friends were behind all this. They
          murdered two people, one of them was my
          boy. Shot him twice in the face, broke
          his wrist too. Tortured everyone there,
          faces mangled, eyes melted, hands
          stabbed. It's awful, bet you didn't know
          your own son could be such a monster.

Officer Monroe lets him go.

                    OFFICER MONROE:
          I didn't know my son had anything to do
          with this.

                    OFFICER THEODORE:
          You lie. You had the invitation that's
          address lead straight to here.

                    OFFICER MONROE:
          I found it at home, at the time I
          thought it was just my son getting
          invited to a party. Making friends, had I
          have known...

                                              (CONTINUED)

CONTINUED:

                    OFFICER THEODORE:
If you had known what? That your sons not
popular enough to get himself invited to
a party. What would have done, stopped
him.
Arrested him.

                    OFFICER MONROE:
And what about you. You knew my son was
somehow involved the moment you found
that letter. The moment you found out
your son was amongst the hostages, what
did you do. You took charge.

                    OFFICER THEODORE:
I done what I had to do to protect my
son.

                    OFFICER MONROE:
My son was there too. That is why you
took control, cause deep down you knew
that maybe my son was behind all this.
Is that why you wanted to be the leader,
to show me who's boss. To kill my own
son.

                    OFFICER THEODORE:
I didn't want to kill anybody.

                    OFFICER MONROE:
I heard about the shoot to kill order
you gave. What was that moments after
you found that letter, would it have
been different if you hadn't found it at
all. You wanted them dead the moment you
found out. So, who was it? The shots,
who did you kill?

                    OFFICER THEODORE:
We didn't kill anybody.

                    OFFICER MONROE:
I know these types of situations, if you
didn't apprehend my son then who did you
take down.

                    OFFICER THEODORE:
No one.

(CONTINUED)

CONTINUED:

                    OFFICER MONROE: WHO WAS
          IT!

                    OFFICER THEODORE:
          I ordered a strike on the teachers ok;
          it was the teachers for fuck sakes. They
          switched roles, pretended to be hostages
          while the teachers came out masked like
          the perps. I issued a kill order on four
          innocent people, all because I wanted to
          save my own son. You were right, I was
          involved in this too emotionally. I had
          clouded judgement and I took four
          people's lives; I won't be able to live
          with that. Those who took the shots won't
          be able to live with that. I ruined
          everything all because of you and your
          stupid fucking son.

                    OFFICER MONROE:
          I told you you'd make a decision you
          would regret. All this because deep down
          you have some deep seeded hatred towards
          me, towards my family. Is it because you
          could never stand up to me in school,
          because I took your girlfriend and made
          her my wife. Because I'm your boss, you
          made an error because you wanted to get
          back at me. You may think my son is a
          monster, but those teacher blood isn't
          on his hands. That's yours, and you have
          to live with that.

                    OFFICER THEODORE:
          I'm going to have your badge for this.

Officer Theodore walks away, wiping the blood from his face.

INT.HOSPITAL - CONTINUOUS.

The ambulance workers are wheeling Stacy into the emergency room.
Doctors come rushing over to help. They tell Miranda she can't
continue past the doors, that she has to wait. Doctors work
helplessly on Stacy.

INT.STACYS HOUSE - KITCHEN - MID DAY.

Stacy is sitting at the table with her little brother. Her father
comes over and hugs and kisses them both. He sits down at the
table and reads the paper. Her mother sets out a bowl of spaghetti
on the table with garlic bread.

                    MOTHER:
          Dig is everybody, dinner is served.

They begin to set out the food provided out on the plates before
them. There comes a knock at the door.

                    FATHER:
          Stacy, would you mind grabbing that.

Stacy jumps up and answers the door. It is the male man, who is a
slight buffer version of brian.

                    BRIAN:
          Special delivery for a Ms. Stacy
          Lawrence.

                    STACY:
          I'm not expecting any package.

                    BRIAN:
          Well, you got a big one here with your
          name on it. I just need your signature
          here and here.

Stacy signs for the package and Brian hands it over to her. Stacy
looks at him confused.

                    STACY:
          Hey, do I know you from somewhere?

                    BRIAN:
          I should hope so, we go to the same
          school together.

                    STACY:
          I think I would have seen a cute boy like
          you running around in my school.

                    BRIAN:
          Just got to open your eyes and take the
          time to get to know me.

                    STACY:
          I hope I get to see you around.

                                              (CONTINUED)

CONTINUED:
                        BRIAN:
              School first thing tomorrow morning. Make
              sure you wake up on time though.

He proceeds to walk away whistling.

                        STACY:
              What do you mean? I'm always up on time.

                        BRIAN:
              Well remember to wake up, it's important
              that you always wake up.

Stacy shuts the door and opens her package, inside is a single
letter. She glances at it and tosses it in the garbage. She goes
back to the table.

                        FATHER:
              Who was that?

                        STACY:
              Just some boy delivering junk mail that's
              all.

                        MOTHER:
              Well, I hope you asked for his number, he
              sounded cute.

                        STACY:
              He was dreamy.

                        BROTHER:
              Ewe gross, Stacy's got a boyfriend.

They all laugh and begin to dig into their food. They are a perfect
family together.

INSERT - GARBAGE CAN - CONTINUOUS.

In the garbage can the letter sits. Written in plain black ink
are the words "Wake up."

INT.EMERGENCY ROOM - CONTINUOUS.

The doctors stand beside the table, sheet drawn over her face.
Blood stains the white blankets and clothes. The doctors look
upset, taking off their masks and gloves. A long blaring noise of
a flat line can be heard coming from the monitor. The lead doctor
looks up at the clock.

                                              (CONTINUED)

CONTINUED:

                    DOCTOR:
          Time of death. 9:42PM.

INT.HOSPITAL - CONTINUOUS.

Police officers come in looking for the two girls. The doctor
gives them the sad news. He points to the waiting room where
Miranda is waiting. When they go in Miranda isn't among the
individuals.

INT.MIRANDAS HOUSE - BATHROOM - CONTINUOUS.

Miranda walks in through the front door as a taxi drives away.
She makes her way into the bathroom and locks the door. Tv can be
heard roaring from the living room and the sound of someone
snoring.

Miranda locks the bathroom door and stares at herself through the
shards in the broken mirror.

                    MIRANDA:
          I'm not like them, I could never be like
          them. I'm the monster that little kids
          fear, I hurt people.
          All I ever wanted was to be your friend,
          and you went and hurt me.

She begins to cry, picking through the garbage she pulls out a
broken piece of glass.

                    MIRANDA:(CONT'D)
          All I ever wanted was to be different.
          To make you like me, love me, adore me. I
          wanted you all to see me as beautiful.
          But all I'll ever be on the outside is
          what I am on the inside. Disgusting. I
          hurt you and inside a part of me died.
          Why do you still hate me, I just wanted
          you to be like me so we could be friends.
          Please don't hate me, I'm sorry. I just
          wanted to be different.

She jumps in the bathtub and takes the piece of glass and slides
it down her wrist. Deep incisions to both wrists, blood quickly
pools in the tub. She drops the glass on the floor and closes her
eyes.

CONTINUED:

                    MIRANDA: (CONT'D)
          But i'll never be different. I'll always
          stay me.

Outside the door pounding can be heard, she can hear someone trying
to get in. It's her mother.

                    MRS.OSTEEN:
          Miranda is everything ok in there. I can
          hear you talking to yourself, let me in.
          Miranda open the door and let me in.

She continues to pound on the door, Miranda doesn't say anything or
move at all.

EXT.WOODS BY THE FARMHOUSE - CONTINUOUS.

Blake and Brian are darting through the heavy thick brush and
branches. Every so often catching a stick in the face, sometimes
tripping and stumbling over logs but never checking to see if
they were okay. They would just get up and keep running. The
sounds of police sirens can be heard, barking from dogs and the
shouts from officers saying which way they went. They are being
tracked.

                    BLAKE:
          Come on don't stop, were almost there.

They make their way through the brush and branch, until they come
into a clearing. Parked is Blakes van, Blake hopes into the
driver's side while Brian jumps into the passenger side. In the
back is all the liquor and funnels that Mike and his gang had
brought to the party. Blake quickly starts up the van keeps the
lights turned off until the reach the main road and past the
trail to the farmhouse where Brians dad is still standing.

They pass several cop cars on the way by, they duck their heads
but its night so the cops can't see in through the windows.

                    BRIAN:
          You think they're going to turn around
          and come back after us?

                    BLAKE:
          They won't be tracking us.

                                                      (CONTINUED)

CONTINUED:

                    BRIAN:
          By now they probably know who we are,
          it's only a matter of time before they
          find out you took your dads van and keep
          an eye out for any make and model
          matching the license plate.

                    BLAKE:
          That's why I switched them off someone
          else's car. Figured if we were going to
          be using my van, I didn't want any
          witnesses giving the description of the
          license plate they saw. That should buy
          us some time.

                    BRIAN:
          Sometime before they catch up with us. If
          not tonight then tomorrow, Blake we
          killed someone today.
          They are not going to stop looking for
          us.

                    BLAKE:
          We were never going to get away with
          this. Sooner or later the law was bound
          to catch up with us, I mean do you
          really think we could have lived the
          rest of our lives knowing what we did. I
          know you said nobody was supposed to die
          tonight but so what, we taught them a
          powerful message. A lesson they couldn't
          learn is school. They'll ask themselves
          for the rest of their lives why did we
          do what we did: the answer, it's because
          we can. It's because we are powerful, we
          are no longer the bullied or tormented.
          Just bask in knowledge knowing we made a
          difference tonight, we became gods.
          Legends among men, just live we that for
          the moment.

Brian is staring out the window, watching as the trees and the
signs go by.

                    BRIAN:
          But I don't think I want to live a
          legend.... Do you think we're going to
          hell?

(CONTINUED)

CONTINUED:

                    BLAKE:
I've been to hell. Hell is waking up
thinking that the suffering in your life
has meaning. You think maybe if I endure
this long enough that there is a lesson
behind it all. Truth to be told, there is
no lesson, no meaning. Sometimes you
just suffer.

                    BRIAN:
I like to think that there is no hell.
That this is all just a bad dream. That
my dad is still the man I believed him to
be.

                    BLAKE:
What do you mean?

                    BRIAN:
Mike told me moments before he shot
Derek, that my father isn't the man I
believed him to be. He bullied Mr.
Theodore all through high school and
work. My dad is the type of person I
despise the most. Fueled by hatred Mikes
father would come home and beat him, a
coward could never stand up to the
person he hated most. Because of my
father, his impact created a monster. If
my father hadn't had done what he done,
maybe Mike wouldn't have pushed me
around, beat you up for being different,
raped Stacy. Because of my dad, we are
in this situation.

                    BLAKE:
Someone once told me that a child's life
is influenced by the nature of their
parents. We don't know if things would
have been different if Mikes dad hadn't
abused him. He could still be that same
monster.

                    BRIAN:
But if he hadn't, all our lives could
have been better.

                    BLAKE:
Not, Mirandas.

CONTINUED:

                    BRIAN:
          Those girls still would have tormented
          her.

                    BLAKE:
          Some people are destined to become
          monsters. There will always be suffering
          in the world. Some people are just
          destined to endure it the most.

The rest of the ride home is quiet, and uncomfortable. They arrive
at Brians house.

INT.BRIANS HOUSE - CONTINUOUS.

Brian and Blake walk in through the front door.

                    BLAKE:
          You should get your things; you don't
          want to be here when the police show up.

                    BRIAN:
          And what are we going to do? Run the
          rest of our lives.

                    BLAKE:
          Go somewhere far away, throw back a few
          pints we got in the back seat. Have
          ourselves a party, our own celebration.

                    BRIAN:
          You think I would want to party with you.
          You killed Mike, you shot Stacy. You said
          it yourself; the law was going to catch
          up with us eventually. I'm not going to
          run, I'm going to turn myself in.

                    BLAKE:
          After all you've been through, you're
          just going to hand yourself over to
          them. Come on, enjoy your freedom while
          you still have it.

                    BRIAN:
          And what about Miranda and Stacy?

CONTINUED:

                    BLAKE:
          The police probably have them in
          custody. Providing Stacy even made it
          through surgery.

                    BRIAN:
          That's what I don't get about you, you
          show no remorse for what you did. I liked
          her, and you just took her away from me.

                    BLAKE:
          And I loved him, don't think for a minute
          that were both not in the same boat here.
          Be thankful I gave you this moment here,
          you could have easily been gunned down
          just like those teachers.

                    BRIAN:
          If I had known that they would die I
          wouldn't have agreed to it. I can't live
          with myself knowing we killed people
          tonight.

                    BLAKE:
          But you could deal with hurting them is
          that it. You know you're a big shot,
          talking about getting revenge and
          teaching lessons. You led this pack like
          a wolf, yet secretly you were just a
          rabbit in a wolfs costume. Should have
          hooped away when you had the chance,
          truthfully, I think you still would have
          caved. We had made it out like it was
          planned, you would have rushed home and
          turned yourself in. You're all weak,
          pathetic, you proved inferior tonight.
          You deserve to be treated the way you've
          always been treated.

Brian reaches for the phone in the kitchen.

                    BRIAN:
          I may be weak but at least I'm doing the
          right thing.

Brian turns his back on Blake and walks into the living room. He
manages to call 911 and presses talk, the operator comes on the
line just as Blake walks up behind Brian.

CONTINUED:

                    OPERATOR:
          This is 911, what seems to be the
          emergency?

                    BRIAN:
          My name is Brian Monroe, I'd like to
          turn myself in....

Blake grabs one of Brians weights and cracks him in the back of
the head with it. The phone falls out of Brians hand, it smashes
on the floor. Brian places his hand on the back of his head,
blood covers his hand. He pulls it away stunned; he turns to look
at Blake.

                    BRIAN:(CONT'D)
          Wh... wh... why?

                    BLAKE:
          I just can't let you turn us in. I still
          have work that needs to be done.

He rushes Brian and they fight, Brian tries his best to fight him
off. They knock over the tv, sending it falling to the floor. They
tear the room apart, eventually Blake has managed to position
himself on top on Brian. He has the weight in his hand, he raises
it above his head.

                    BLAKE:(CONT'D)
          I still have never accepted your
          apology.

He brings the weight down on Brians face, he continues to smash.
Blood and bone go everywhere, Brians face is completely caved in
and unrecognizable. Blake drops the weight and stands up; he walks
out onto the street and takes out Stacy's phone that he still has
in his pocket. He sends a message to the number from before.

INSERT-PHONE - CONTINUOUS.

Message reads, 'we need to talk now."

A respond message reads, 'Great, meet me at the school.'

EXT.BOTTOM OF THE TRAIL - CONTINUOUS.

Officer Monroe is still waiting when his phone goes off, he grabs
it without looking at who is calling.

CONTINUED:

                    OFFICER MONROE:
          Brian?

The secretary is on the other end.

                    SECRETARY:
          No, its Cindy.

                    OFFICER MONROE:
          Oh, I thought it was my son calling.
          What do you want?

                    SECRETARY:
          We had a 911 call that came your house.
          It's your son, he called you turn himself
          in.

                    OFFICER MONROE:
          Is he still there?

                    SECRETARY:
          The operator said there was a loud thud,
          and the phone went dead. What's going on?

Officer Monroe hangs up without answering, he jumps into his car
and speeds off back towards town.

EXT.FARMHOUSE - CONTINUOUS.

Officer Theodore is still ordering officers around. There are six
body bags laid out in front. The surviving victims have all been
taken to the hospitals. The swat leader comes up Officer
Theodore.

                    OFFICER THEODORE:
          Did you manage to find them yet.

                    SWAT LEADER:
          No sir, officers at the hospital report
          that the young girl Ms. Lawrence didn't
          survive surgery. 911 call was called in
          by Mrs. Osteen, apparently Miranda went
          home and slashed her own wrists. Time
          help arrived the girl had long since
          expired.

                    OFFICER THEODORE:
          Any word on the other two?

CONTINUED:
                    SWAT LEADER:
          Not yet, we're still searching. Every
          available unit is out looking for them.
          There's something you need to know?

                  OFFICER THEODORE:
          What is it?

                    SWAT LEADER:
          The farmhouse, we looked into permits and
          foundation records and we stumbled across
          this.

He hands the officer a piece of paper with a name on it.

                    SWAT LEADER:
          That's the name of the person who owns
          this place.

                  OFFICER THEODORE:
          You got to be fucking shitting me.

                    SWAT LEADER:
          Do you know him?

                  OFFICER THEODORE:
          Looks like we're descending further into
          the rabbit hole boys. Gear up I think I
          know where they are going.

INT.SILVERCREEK SCHOOL - PRINCIPALS OFFICE - CONTINUOUS.

Blake has found the school door unlocked; he wanders through the
halls until he comes across the principal's office. The door is
unlocked, and Blake allows himself in. The room is dark, the shades
on the windows are drawn to keep any of the streetlights or
moonlight from coming in. There is someone sitting in the Chair, a
ghostly figure. Blake turns the lights on, and he stands there
surprised.

                    BLAKE:
          It was you; you were behind all this.

Vice-Principal Chandler Grieves is sitting, his hands folded upon
his chest. He too is surprised.

                  MR. GRIEVES:
          When you texted, me I had been expecting
          someone else. Where are the others.

                                                      (CONTINUED)

CONTINUED:

                    BLAKE:
          Dead, well one is. I can't speak for the
          others. Your puppet is laid up in the
          hospital, shot gun to the chest.

                    MR. GRIEVES:
          Stacy was shot. By whom?

                    BLAKE:
          By me, couldn't stand a traitor in our
          group.

                    MR. GRIEVES:
          Such a shame, I had thought better of
          you. Figured you would all work together,
          work on the bigger picture you were
          presented with.

                    BLAKE:
          Is that why you sent me a picture of
          Brian putting that letter in Derek's
          locker.

Mr. Grieves motions for Blake to sit.

                    MR. GRIEVES:
          So, you got that did you. Please have a
          seat.

Blake does.

                    MR. GRIEVES:(CONT'D)
          I can tell you're upset; things didn't
          go two well for Derek did they.

                    BLAKE:
          They went as well as you had planned
          them to. What was it, you got them to
          invite Derek to come. Force tension
          between all of us, Derek gets shot. You
          hope I snap, kill the hostages, then send
          me the video of Brian. Everything goes
          spiraling out of control and I kill them,
          we all die maybe some of us live.
          Whatever the outcome you planned for
          there to be casualties.

                    MR. GRIEVES:
          It's not like that.

                                              (CONTINUED)

CONTINUED:
                    BLAKE:
          Then tell me what it is like.

FLASHBACK - SILVERCREEK SCHOOL - PRINCIPALS OFFICE - YESTERDAY -
MORNING.

Chandler Grieves is sitting by the door, he is hearing the
conversation between Stacy and the principal.

                    STACY:
          You're a monster, you don't want to help
          me at all.

                    PRINCIPAL GOLDSTEIN:
          Ah don't be like that, come on. Do you
          want my help or not?

Stacy storms off out of the office, crying, screaming.

                    STACY:
          You disgusting pig, get away from me.

Principal Goldstein runs after her but stops, she has left. He
turns towards the vice principal who is staring at him, confused.

                    PRINCIPAL GOLDSTEIN:
          What the fuck are you looking at? Get
          back to work.

He walks back into his office and slams the door. Mr. Grieves
follows Stacy outside to the benches. She looks up at him.

                    STACY:
          I suppose you want to help me too.

                    MR. GRIEVES:
          I do, but not in the way he does. I heard
          everything and frankly it disgusts me. I
          can help you.

                    STACY:
          Ya I've heard that one before, I don't
          need your help.

                    MR. GRIEVES:
          I think you're going to want to listen.
          What would you say if for one night I
          could help you get revenge on those that
          hurt you. Would you like to have the
          opportunity to hurt them.

CONTINUED:

                    STACY:
More than anything in the world.

                    MR. GRIEVES:
Take my hand, let's go somewhere private and
talk.

                    STACY:
There's to many of them for me to take on, I
can't do it alone.

                    MR. GRIEVES:
I think I have got a few people that would be
interested in helping you in your cause.

They walk off and head in the direction of the field which is now empty.

FLASHBACK - SILVERCREEK SCHOOL - HALLS - YESTERDAY - NIGHT.

Chandler Grieves dresses up in his mask and gloves. He unlocks the school door
and disarms the security code. He begins placing the letters into the lockers.

FLASHBACK - SILVERCREEK SCHOOL - PRINCIPALS OFFICE - YESTERDAY - NIGHT.

Chandler Grieves dumps a foreign powder into the teacher's coffee. He takes a
cup over to the table and sets four cups around the table. In comes the
principal and the other three teachers.

FLASHBACK - INT. FARMHOUSE - YESTERDAY - NIGHT.

He pulls the unconscious body of the principal and places him in the middle of
the room with the others. He begins tying them up.

FLASHBACK - SCILVERCREEK SCHOOL - HALLS - MORNING.

Chandler Grieves hands Stacy the letter, she folds it up and puts it in her
pocket.

                    MR. GRIEVES:
Make sure you give this to Mr. Monroe. Tell him
he needs to put it into Derek Grants locker.

                    STACY:
Why Derek? We're not supposed to involve him.

                    MR. GRIEVES:
For this to happen you need to invite him. Make
sure you get Brian to do it, you don't need to
have this on your hands.

                    STACY:
What are the extra copies for?

                    MR. GRIEVES:
Just in case you think of anyone else

that needs to be punished.

(CONTINUED)

Stacy leaves and Mr. Grieves goes back to his office and to the
security room. He watches on the monitors as Stacy hands the
invitations to Brian, Brian takes one and goes down the hallway.
He takes one of the invites and slips it into Derek's locker.

END OF FLASHBACK

INT.SILVERCREEK SCHOOL - PRINCIPALS OFFICE - CONTINUOUS.

                    BLAKE:
          That still doesn't explain why you made
          Derek involved in the first place.

                    MR. GRIEVES:
          Cause he needs to suffer just as much as
          the rest. Hanging with the popular kids,
          chilling with kids like you. That
          arrogant attitude, saying I respect
          everyone, and they respect me. I'm a
          friend to all.
          Please, people like that are the worst
          kind of all, you don't hang with one
          person and go play ball with someone who
          just kicked the shit out of them. If I
          had it my way everyone in this school
          that was the likes of them would be dead
          by now, but I just stuck with the worst.

                    BLAKE:
          Derek was different, he wouldn't have
          hurt anyone. He wasn't like Mike; he
          was my friend.

                    MR. GRIEVES:
          Given time he would have, you're lucky he
          never betrayed you sooner. I saved you
          from the suffering.

                    BLAKE:
          Suffering, you had four children do your
          dirty work. You choose the weak, why?

                    MR. GRIEVES:
          Cause I knew you four wanted them dead
          just like me. I planned it for years,
          bought a farmhouse just to

                              (MORE)

                                        (CONTINUED)

CONTINUED:

                    MR. GRIEVES: (cont'd)
          take my victims. Bury their bodies in
          shallow graves, but why should I get my
          hands bloody when you hated them as much
          as I did. I wanted to protect my
          students from being hurt, but I instead
          offered you the chance to redeem
          yourselves.

                    BLAKE:
          So, you sent us in there to kill one
          another. The video of Brian, that was
          all a plan for us to murder each other.
          What for? Were you worried that it be
          traced back to you.

                    MR. GRIEVES:
          I stopped myself from becoming a
          monster, I allowed you to take my place.
          I couldn't just let you all leave
          without killing anyone. Your idea of
          harming them, that nobody was to be
          killed. It's bullshit, you wanted to
          kill, you just needed a little
          motivation. Everyone dies, it was always
          supposed to end that way.

                    BLAKE:
          And the teachers, what about them?

FLASHBACK - FARMHOUSE - YESTERDAY - NGHT.

A car pulls up to the front of the house. The four teachers have
all carpooled and are now getting out and entering the barn, they
are looking at their phones.

The lights are on, the teachers gaze up and around their
surroundings. In the center of the room of the room, is four
chairs and the equipment that they will be used to be tied up
with.

Joel Simmons digs through the bag and pulls out one of the black
hooded bags.

                    MR. SIMMONS:
          All kind of unnecessary for a teachers
          meeting don't you think.

CONTINUED:

                    MRS.WINTERS:
          I first thought that when we had to drive
          all the way out here.

The four of them begin to choke but never make it to the door,
the drug has finally kicked in. As they fall and begin to pass
out Chandler Grieves comes in wearing his mask holding up a cloth
under the mask to protect his face from the fumes. He begins
dragging them to the chairs and sitting them upright.

END OF FLASHBACK.

INT.SILVERCREEK SCHOOL - PRINCIPALS OFFICE - CONTINUOUS.

                    MR. GRIEVES:
          I put the teachers in there in the hope
          that you would take care of them as
          well.

He flips on the live stream video he has on the computer.

                    MR. GRIEVES:(CONT'D)
          By the looks of it I say you took care
          of them quite well. Quite the ordeal
          isn't it, the situation is being
          broadcast all over the news.

                    BLAKE:
          Oh, is it. Didn't think we make the news
          that fast. So why the teachers?

                    MR. GRIEVES:
          Because they caused everyone as much
          harm as those students did. Suppose to
          be a beacon of hope, that's what you are
          when you take this job. Day in and day
          out, those teachers would treat students
          like shit. Half the time they started
          everything, always sitting back
          watching. It sickening watching students
          come in here crying and all they get in
          punished for what:

                         (MORE)

                                        (CONTINUED)

CONTINUED:

                    MR. GRIEVES: (cont'd)
          defending themselves. While the bullies
          get a slap on the wrist. Students torment
          slash their wrists or put guns in their
          mouths and were supposed to help them
          from getting to that point. But all that
          four did was reach over and help pull
          the trigger. Students were nothing but a
          paycheck to them.

Chandler Grieves looks at his watch.

                    MR. GRIEVES:(CONT'D)
          It's getting late, you should probably
          go, I imagine the police will be here
          soon. That's if you don't want to get
          caught.

                    BLAKE:
          They're coming here cause that farmhouse
          is in your name, it'll be traced back to
          you. That means that the police will come
          after you as well, that's evidence right
          there that you were behind all this.

                    MR. GRIEVES:
          And why would they come after me. It's
          just in my name, I could tell them you
          were trying to frame me or that this was
          all a misunderstanding, it just so
          happened my farmhouse was used for an
          act of violence tonight. They have no
          evidence that places me at the scene that
          I was behind this all. Unless you're here
          to kill me I suggest you move along I
          think I can hear the sirens coming now.

Blake gets up to leave, but before he exits, he turns around.

                    BLAKE:
          I won't kill you; you'll get what's
          coming to you soon enough.

Blake leaves, the vice principal continues to sit there and watch
the live stream of the incident.

INT.BRIANS HOUSE - CONTINUOUS.

Officer Monroe pulls up to his house and gets out. He notices
that the door is still open. He rushes inside and draws his side
arm.

                    OFFICER MONROE:
          Brian! Brian! Brian where are you.

He enters in through the front door and drops his side arm, he
notices the wreck. Tv smashed, Treadmill turned over, lamps stand
toppled over. In the middle of the living room floor is Brian.
Blood soaks the carpet, the blood-stained weight left by his
head. Officer Monroe rushes over and lifts his son in his arms,
cradling the mess left of his head in his arms. He buries his
face into his chest, covering his face in blood and tears. He
mourns just as two officers walk through the front door: guns
drawn. They holster them when they see what has happened.

INT.SILVERCREEK SCHOOL - PRINCIPALS OFFICE - CONTINUOUS.

Officers burst through the door, as Mr. Grieves sits in his chair,
head slumped over. Blood splattered on the ceiling, staining the
desk. A pistol fell by his side. A single note on the desk says,
"Took you long enough, you just missed him" It is written on the
invitation.

INT.BLAKES HOUSE - LIVING ROOM - CONTINUOUS.

Blakes dad is passed out on the couch, snoring. He is carrying in
the chug funnel from the back of the van. He ties his father's
wrists and legs to the rocking chair, once secured he slaps him
awake.

His father snaps too.

                    FATHER:
          What's the meaning of this, you looking
          for another beating.

                    BLAKE:
          No, I just came home to see you one last
          time.

The father notices his arm and legs are tied. He tries to wiggle
himself free but cant.

CONTINUED:

                    FATHER:
          You untie me right now you son of a
          bitch.

                    BLAKE:
          I never understand why you keep calling
          her that, is that why she left you
          because you have no respect for woman.

                    FATHER:
          No, she left me cause she's a fucking
          whore and her sons a god damn faggot.

                    BLAKE:
          See I don't think you're in the position
          to be saying such things. If I were you,
          I'd be scared right about now.

He turns the channel to the news where they are broadcasting the
situation.

                    NEWS REPORTER:
          It appears four individuals tortured and
          even murdered some of their fellow
          classmates. Now we don't know the whole
          story just yet...

Blake turns down the volume. His image along with three others
are displayed across the screen.

                    FATHER:
          So, you finally snapped did you, come
          home to do your old man in as well.

                    BLAKE:
          I just wanted you to finally see the
          true me, after all you had a hand in all
          this. All those beatings shaped me into
          what you see before you.

                    FATHER:
          Always knew you were a coward; can't take
          your old man in a fight you have to hold
          him down and torture him is that it.

CONTINUED:
                    BLAKE:
          Yes I'm the one who's a coward. This is
          coming from a man who came home drunk
          every night and beat his son. His own
          child. Couldn't find someone your own
          age at the bar so you had to beat me. I
          used to lie awake at night hoping you
          wouldn't come home, maybe you're at the
          drunk tank maybe you're lying dead
          behind the bar alley. Truth be told I
          didn't care what happened to you just as
          long as you never made it home.

Blake heads to the kitchen and grabs a jug from under the counter,
he fills up the funnel until the tube is filled to the top in a
green liquid. He come back with at and hold it out in front of his
dad.

                    BLAKE:(CONT'D)
          I came back because I wanted to play a
          game with my father, it's a drinking
          game. If you finish this I'll let you go
          and you'll never see me again. Do we
          have a deal?

                    FATHER:
          Go to hell!

                    BLAKE:
          You know a friend asked me once tonight,
          he wondered if we were all going there.
          Sure, I am, but not before you go.

He sticks the tube in his father's mouth and flips the valve. The
green liquid runs out and into his mouth, some pours past his
chin the rest he swallows.

                    BLAKE:(CONT'D)
          There we go, drink up. Figured you're so
          used to drinking beer I give you
          something else to drink. Drain cleaner,
          cleans drains maybe it clean scrub out
          the bile liquid you constantly got
          flowing through you. Or it could just
          kill you.

His father started to puke, blood and a white yellow bile shot
past the tube and onto the floor and his shirt. He makes a
choking sound; he can't breathe he just continues to puke.

CONTINUED:

Blake drops the funnel and sits down on the chair across from
him. He flips through the channels on the tv while his father
next to him dies. Sirens come on and lights are flashing in the
yard. Blake dusts of his clothes and turns off the tv, he gives
his dead father a kiss on the head and closes his eyes for him.
He then places his hands on his head and walks outside.

INT.POLICE STATION - INTERROGATION ROOM - CONTINUOUS.

Blake is sitting at the table, his hands cuffed and chained to it.
Officer Monroe and Theodore walk into the room, they lay images of
the scene out before him. One is of Brian and the other is of Mike.

                    BLAKE:
          You can put those away I know what I
          did.

                    OFFICER THEODORE:
          I want you take a long hard look at
          these; you killed my boy. Why did you
          kill him?

                    BLAKE:
          Because your son isn't as innocent as you
          may think he is. He caused all this,
          because of him and his gang and his
          girlfriend and her whores they caused us
          pain. So, we infected it back.

                    OFFICER THEODORE:
          Pain, you want to talk about pain.
          Because of you, my boy will never get to
          graduate. The rest of them will never get
          to live a normal life.

                    BLAKE:
          And you want to blame me, if I recall
          Officer Monroe's son here was in on it
          too.

                    OFFICER MONROE:
          And he's dead because of you too.

                    BLAKE:
          How do you know it was me? Could have
          been the other girl who did it.

                                              (CONTINUED)

CONTINUED:

                    OFFICER MONROE:
          We know it was you because the other two
          are dead. One slit her wrists, the other
          dead from her gunshot wound.

                    BLAKE:
          Pity, though the fat one should have
          lasted longer.

                    OFFICER MONROE:
          Why did you kill my son, if he helped you
          why did you turn against him.

                    BLAKE:
          Because I had unfinished work to be done,
          if you must know he wanted to turn
          himself in. I just couldn't allow that
          to happen.

                    OFFICER THEODORE:
          Enough! Tell us why you did all this,
          why the teachers? Why the students?

                    BLAKE:
          For me to tell you I first need to show
          you. Go get me my phones you took off
          me.

Officer Theodore steps outside and comes back with an evidence
bag with two phones in it.

                    BLAKE:(CONT'D)
          Now I know that is evidence so I'm not
          supposed to touch it. I'll let you do the
          honor but if you open my phone, the black
          one. There should be a video on there.

Officer Theodore plays the video of the two boys have sex.

                    OFFICER THEODORE:
          What is this disgusting shit?

                    BLAKE:
          Sorry for the wrong video, damn shame
          really. Too bad nobody will get to see
          that, they were rising stars in the film
          industry. But seriously go to the other
          video.

CONTINUED:

Officer Theodore played the video of Stacy's rape. Officer Monroe
leans over to check the video himself.

                    OFFICER MONROE:
          That's Ms. Lawrence, one of the unsubs in
          the case.

                    OFFICER THEODORE:
          You mind telling us what we're watching
          here.

                    BLAKE:
          That my friends is a homemade rape
          video. The four individuals involved
          including the camera man are as follows:
          Chris Cook, John Adams, Henry Rush and
          your son Mike Theodore.

                    OFFICER THEODORE:
          This isn't my son he wouldn't be involved
          in such filth.

                    BLAKE:
          Oh, but that is him, skip forward when
          he starts talking you will be able to
          recognize his voice. This right here is
          one reason why we did what we did, they
          beat Brian in the shower make fun of
          people cause their gay and fat. By no
          means is your son and his friends the
          victims here, were not the only monsters
          out there you know.

Officer Theodore places the phones back into the bag.

                    OFFICER MONROE:
          So, you did all this because they were
          bullies.

                    BLAKE:
          No, we did all this because we could.
          Because they let us. We asserted our
          power and our dominance, and we came out
          on top.

                    OFFICER THEODORE:
          The local of the house, we traced that
          back to your vice-principal. You want to
          explain why he was of importance in
          this.

                                        (CONTINUED)

CONTINUED:
                    BLAKE:
          Look through the other phone, you'll
          find a number on the other, A
          conversation between Stacy and the vice
          principal. He organized this whole thing
          you know. Thinks he can get away with it.
          That number should be enough
          incriminating evidence to have him
          arrested.

                    OFFICER THEODORE:
          You never did say why you killed my son,
          why him and leave the others.

                    BLAKE:
          We were never supposed to kill anybody,
          we couldn't stress that enough. Just hurt
          that was all, but the other boy who died.

                    OFFICER MONROE:
          What other boy.

                    BLAKE:
          Don't play dumb, the other boy the one
          neither of you have mentioned. His name
          was Derek Grant, he was my friend. And
          Mike shot him, everything was going to
          plan then Mike got a gun and shot him.
          Died instantly, your son didn't mean to,
          the bullet was meant for me but still.
          That didn't stop me from putting two
          holes in his head. I guess you could say
          things after that just spiraled out of
          control.

                    OFFICER THEODORE:
          I've heard enough, first you excuse my
          son of being a rapist and then you call
          him a murderer.

Officer Theodore gets up to leave.

                    BLAKE:
          You're going to want to stay and listen
          to what else I have to say. And if you
          think about deleting that video I'd have
          you know that it's all over the school.
          I'm sure someone would be happy to
          supply Officer Monroe here with the
          video if he asked for it.

                                              (CONTINUED)

CONTINUED:

                    OFFICER THEODORE:
Okay I'm listening to what else do you
want to say.

                    BLAKE:
The teacher weren't our idea, frankly
they weren't even a part of our agenda.

                    OFFICER MONROE:
But you still used them to escape.

                    BLAKE:
I didn't think that was going to work.
But it did, and we didn't even have to
kill them. You did that for us. It's
weird seeing you two in a room together.

                    OFFICER MONROE:
Why's that?

                    BLAKE:
After what your son told me. How you two
fought in school, and now even at work
you can't see eye to eye. Officer
Theodore here used to go home and beat
his son. I'll never understand what
drives a man to hurt his own flesh and
blood.
Maybe that's why Mike and me are so
damaged, improperly raised. So, Mike
beats Brian, hurts many others all
because he is abused by his daddy. It's
kind of a vicious circle really, two
adults at a war for years one beats his
son, and that son beats the other man's
son.
Really comes back to bite you in the ass
doesn't it, how your constant fighting
is what landed your children in that
situation in the first place.

                    OFFICER THEODORE:
So, you're blaming me for my son's death!

                    BLAKE:
I'm blaming both of you. Do you hate each
other so much that you killed four
innocent people just to get back at him.
                    (MORE)

CONTINUED:

                    BLAKE: (cont'd)

                    Judging by your expression I
          take that as a yes, you hated him so
          much that you just wanted to put a
          bullet between his sons' eyes and call
          it justice. And to think the reason I
          went out there with the
          teachers was on a whim, thought you would
          pull the trigger just because you were
          eager enough to get your son out of
          there. Little did I know the true reason
          behind it all.

Officer Theodore slams his hands on the desk.

                    OFFICER THEODORE:
          How dare you blame us for what happened.
          You're a twisted fuck that's going to be
          locked up for a long time, you should
          have run while you had the chance.

MONTAGE - VARIOUS LOCATIONS

-- We see Serena walk into a restaurant in the middle of the day.
She has her hood drawn up over her head. People stop at glare at
her face. People are whispering and laughing, some talking about
how hideous she now looks. She sits down at the table. The waiter
from the beginning comes to wait on her.

-- Kelsey is in her room trying to sleep, she tosses and turns
from nightmares. She goes to the bathroom and looks at the mark
left on her hand. She takes a bottle of pills from the cabinet and
downs her bottle of anti-depressants. Her mother comes in and
finds her overdosing on the bathroom floor.

-- Jennie walks the school halls, she's in a wheelchair. Foot was
amputated. People laugh at her disfigurement. She tries to tell
them to stop but can't make the words to do so.

-- Chris is walking the streets wearing glasses. He has a walking
stick and a seeing eye dog. Two officers approach him, they take
him by the arms and escort him to their car.

--Henry and John are in a meeting for victims of sexual abuse.
Officers come in and escort them from the group..

CONTINUED:

-- On the fields of the school football and cheerleading is still going on. New teachers have taken the lead, also new members to the team.

-- Officer Monroe sits at home; he is wearing tattered worn-out dirty clothes. He drinks a glass of scotch and admires his service pistol. He takes his badge and tosses it in the trash.

-- Officer Theodore is fighting with his wife at home, arguing over the funeral details. He punches a hole in his wall in frustration.

                    BLAKE:(V.O)
          You may have caught me and that's fine,
          I know my time is almost up. I'll never
          make it in prison, but at least I did
          one final thing in my life. We were
          punished, beaten, bullied, the tormented
          but we became something more. We became
          something more; some will call us legends
          for what we did. We have become zealots
          of a cause, an image to be worshiped.
          The media will idolize us, we will be
          known as the people who became the
          tormentor's torment. Oh, sure we ruined
          some lives, but we did it because we
          could. There's nothing left you can do,
          take me down and more will rise there
          are so much more like us out there just
          waiting for a sign to come. Why go home
          and overdose on pills or blow your own
          brains out, what will that get you. A
          page in the back of the yearbook, no we
          need something more. I'm not going to
          die a coward or a monster, I'm going to
          die a fucking icon.

END OF MONTAGE.

BACK TO SCENE.

EXT.POLICE STATION - MID DAY.

Blake is being escorted out of the building Officer #1 and Officer
#2. He is in his red jumpsuit, with cuffs and chains around his
hands and feet. They bring him down the steps and news reporters
crowd him, sticking microphones in his face but the officers shove
him to the side.

In amongst the crowd is Officer Monroe, he is wearing the same
clothes as the Montage. There is also Officer Theodore as well,
Kelsey's mother can be seen tears in her eyes. Other people can
be seen as well, everyone has a somber hateful look upon their
face. They all seem to be reaching for something out of their
pockets.

Blake smiles as they slowly approach him, he looks forward and
sees Derek standing there.

                    BLAKE:
          Wait for me.

Derek turns his back and starts to walk away; Blake closes his
eyes. As everything around him goes dark a gunshot can be heard
and the screams of others follow.

INT.HOUSE - BEDROOM - CONTINUOUS.

A young man is sitting on his bedroom floor, he is loading a
handgun with the bullets he has laid out on the floor. He looks
up at his tv screen and sees the news report of the incident from
the night before. The news reporter is giving details on what
happened, as the four individuals involved in the pictures appear
on the screen. The young man turns off the tv and loads the
cartridge into the gun, he clicks the safety off.